Sarah – Searching For Love

A Collie Press book

Copyright © Frank Melling 2025

First published in Great Britain in 2025 by:
The Collie Press
Manley Lane, Manley, Cheshire WA6 0PB.

The right of Frank Melling to be identified as the author of this Work has been asserted by him in accordance with the Copyright, Designs and Patents Act 1988.

Text and Design © Frank Melling
Editor: Carol Melling
Cover design: © Frank Melling
Typesetting: Geoff Fisher

All Rights Reserved. No part of this publication may be reproduced, stored in a retrieval system, or transmitted in any form, or by any means, electronic, mechanical, photocopying, recording or otherwise without the prior permission in writing of the copyright holder, nor be otherwise circulated in any form or binding or cover, other than that in which it is published and without a similar condition being imposed upon the subsequent publisher.

All enquiries should be addressed to the publisher.

This is a work of fiction. Names, characters, businesses, places, events, locales, and incidents are either products of the author's imagination or used in a fictitious manner. Any resemblance to actual persons, living or dead, or actual events is purely coincidental.

ISBN 978-1-7384300-1-7

A CIP catalogue record for this book is available in the British Library

Printed and bound by CPI Antony Rowe

See Frank Melling's other books at

www.frankmelling.co.uk

Introduction and thanks

I decided to write *Sarah – Searching For Love* after chatting to a lady at a Christmas fair we attended. Only an author could say that without getting into trouble at home!

Without knowing it she represented so many other women in the modern world that I had to write not so much her specific story but something about all the decent people who try to fall in love with someone worthy of them, but never quite manage it.

That's Sarah's story.

Ironically, the more opportunities there are to find life partners, the harder it seems to be for things to work out.

I also wanted to write about real women – not game-show parodies of the people I meet. So Sarah is a complete woman in every way – in terms of intellect, judgement, courage, and appearance. She's not some super-duper-woman in a sparkly bodysuit carrying lightning bolts in her handbag, but just a thoroughly nice person wanting life to work out for her.

Is that too much to ask? I didn't think so...

As for writing in a woman's voice, this was challenging but no more so than writing as an AI, or a caretaker working for the Devil in Perdition, as I have done in other stories.

Equally, I needed to take care that I reflected what women like Sarah might actually think and say.

I am grateful for the help given to me by the test readers of the book, particularly Maureen and my wife Carol, who is also my editor and best friend.

The truth is that I wouldn't have written Sarah without her support – emotionally and professionally!

As with all our books, *Sarah* has been typeset by Geoff Fisher – a fine, old-fashioned craftsman – and I am very grateful for his skill in making the book look so well produced.

If Geoff is a traditional craftsman, then at the other end of the time scale is ChatGPT, the AI which designed the covers – but didn't write any of the book!

Working with this machine entity was fascinating — it showed what can be done when humans and machines co-operate.

Finally, a thanks to CPI at Melksham. CPI are one of the biggest book printers in Britain, but Tara and Claire always give me the impression that our book is the most important one they have ever printed – and that means so much to me, as it does to any author publishing their own book.

I have had a lot of fun writing *Sarah's* story – and I hope you enjoy following her search for love, bumpy road though it is.

CHAPTER ONE

I looked in the mirror and didn't like what I saw.

I had a decent job, a decent house, a decent car and decent friends. In fact, I had more than most 34 year olds in the country.

But what I didn't have was that special person everyone needs at the centre of their life. Someone you look at and think, "I'm so glad I'm with you."

And he looks back at you, and gives you a little kiss and a smile because he believes it too.

I used to think that I had someone like this but the truth was that he was so much better in my imagination than he was in real life, because he turned out to be a grade "A" bastard.

Brandon - with a capital B for Bastard.

Brandon - the history teacher, on his way to becoming a Head of Department.

All smiling Brandon - at the staff Christmas party.

Bone idle Brandon - who did sod all around the house because he was always busy with his school work.

And, worst of all, thieving Brandon - who I caught going through my purse.

But even having to kick him out didn't stop the longing.

I tucked my legs underneath me, emptied some tonic into a large tumbler and tipped in the gin. Then I looked at the glass – shrugged my shoulders and, as usual, added another generous slug.

G&T anaesthetic – for yet another bloody awful 24 hours of my life.

It had been one of those days – the sort of days which were normal now.

The next thing was normal too – night after night.

I could never get really comfortable with what I was going to do next. I mean, I wasn't being forced or anything but sitting in my pyjamas and then starting always made me fidget. Perhaps you never get over being taught by nuns.

Shit! I still had do it! It was as if some ghoul was summoning me to my iPad. I switched it on and took a deep breath.

One click later and a familiar picture appeared – accompanied by slightly urgent music which was calling me to action.

Not that I needed telling. Time was getting shorter by the day!

The screen always showed a couple in their late twenties, walking through a sun dappled wood along with their golden Labrador, pink tongue hanging out and eager to please.

She is super slim, obviously, with long, dark brown hair hanging casually, but immaculately, over her crisp, white blouse.

Gazing down at her admiringly, wonderingly even at his immense good fortune, is a slightly older man with designer stubble and fashionably groomed hair.

His denim shirt is rolled back above his elbows revealing a hint of crisp biceps to perfectly match his action man looks.

Then, almost immediately, the standard request popped up on screen.

I hesitated. More and more, I thought what's the point? It was a question that was getting more difficult to answer as each day went by.

The prompt said:

Please enter your name.

I was a fast two-finger typist: Sarah Bersham.

Password – Please use upper and lower case letters and a symbol: Doomedgirl!

Every night I stopped and thought of where I was in life, who I was, what I was – and I always hated the answers.

Sarah Bersham: Bloody regular user of "More Than Friends Dating".

Aged 34; split up two years ago from a long term relationship (and I thought I was actually his bloody partner, whatever that means!) because I couldn't trust him; no children; brown hair with a few grey streaks here and there; some eye wrinkles – especially after a bad night's sleep; used to be a size 12 with no problem but now a very tight 14; shops for clothes in Next; liked skiing but stopped going because my ex was a wimp; enjoys walking – proper walking not messing about ambling round a garden centre on a Sunday afternoon; full time job as a junior manager in customer support; drives a four year old Mini Clubman; own house with parking outside and a south facing garden; seeks similar male for friendship and maybe more… (and be bloody quick about it too because I'm not getting any younger - but not too quick because every bloke which fate has offered up so far has been a clone of my ex-partner and I've got the t-shirt for that experience!)

I looked at my picture on the site. They were always asking me to update it and the last try had not been good.

I should never have worn pants that tight – and with my top tucked in too!

The roll of fat showed.

Bloody hell! How it showed! It was if the line of flesh above my jeans was going to invade my legs all the way down to my knees – like some alien monster growing bigger as it gobbled me up on its way to my feet.

And the smile! Had someone superglued wrinkles on my face? Christ, I didn't really look like that, did I?

At least every man out there knew I wasn't cat fishing. No AI would make anyone look so gross!

My bloke filter came on automatically the moment I logged on but the truth was that the older I got the more active the filter became. At Uni, it was "Does he look fit and washed?" Alongside the mental check that I had taken my pill that morning.

Now, it was a lot harder. Ten minutes in bed followed by a quick clean with a baby wipe was not enough.

I needed so much more from a man. Yes - a man, not a randy

20 year old with only one thing on his mind. Not that I didn't need that as well!

I wanted someone to like me – fancy me too, of course, but more than just look at my bum and boobs. I wanted someone to look at my face and think – and, well, think nice thoughts about me because I looked worth being with.

I cleared my head and went into full bloke filtering mode:

No – I don't like kids and I'm sorry your wife died of cancer.

No – I don't want to go for a round the world trip on a motorbike with some bloke I don't know.

No – You're not Special Forces – nice picture though – and no I'm not sending you any ransom money so that you can escape from the Taliban.

No!

No!

No!

No!

No!

It was hard work. I reached for another tin of tonic and looked accusingly at the bottle of gin which was now only half full.

CHAPTER TWO

My dad always says I'm a trier. Whatever I'm doing I'll give it my best shot – always.

After the customary exchange of messages, and I really did know the whole system very well by now, we met in Burlington's Fine Coffee Emporium.

I chose a skinny latte and cherry muffin. I wanted the sugar and fat hit of the cherry muffin so badly because these meetings were always high stress. I knew I was lying to myself but I thought that I could, maybe, claw back the calories by skipping gin for the next two nights: maybe.

I found a table next to the wall, where there wasn't as much passing traffic, and sat down whilst he went to get our coffees and muffins. We'd both been on time which was a good, neutral start. Even so, the first thing I did was to take a long look at the man and begin the evaluation.

It had to be done, I knew it had, but becoming a professional date assessor was not where I had seen myself ten years ago.

Okay, here we go.

Simon Holt: New user of "More Than Friends Dating".

Aged 40 – and he actually was because I had checked his profile on LinkedIn; divorced – I would have checked this too but his Facebook page was private; tallish - but not like a rugby player or anything; hair - sort of browny-grey and a bit mousy coloured; quite clear laughter lines because he used to laugh a lot but not so much now; used to be quite a good tennis player and won the doubles' class at the club tournament with his then new wife but doesn't bother anymore; plans and then arranges the installation of industrial robots in factories and so has a 3 Series BMW company car but with cloth seats, not leather; fed up with blind dates and nights out with women he doesn't really like but goes through the motions out of a sense of duty to society; seeks someone to like who can be a friend; will not, and dare not, mention the "L" word.

He returned and sat down.

It was appalling how good I had become at the process of bloke grading even in the first few minutes. I ran through the standard check list at lightning speed. Forget AI – I was miles better.

Was the picture he had sent honest? Yes, more or less, it was. In fact, he was actually better in the flesh than the picture on the website and that was rare!

Did he smell? You'd be surprised how many men turn up having forgotten their deodorant.

Was he reasonably dressed? Not flashy because this would be too much pressure and you'd have to watch how you looked all the time but, you know, reasonable and decent enough to be seen out in public.

Did he smile? A nice smile which said there was a decent sort of person living inside his head?

Was he some political looney? Left or right, it didn't matter – just as long as he wasn't going to batter her to death with his view of the world.

Did he have 'I disease'? "I did this and I did that and I'm going to…"

And what about me?

"Oh you, well you're only the audience…"

I smiled – not too much because I didn't want him to get the idea that I was too keen, but enough to tell him I wasn't about to start looking at my phone and making excuses about having to visit my Nanna in Wrexham.

"Do you fancy another one?"

Did he?

He'd been careful to stay away from talking too much about

work – industrial robotic painting arms being more than a turn off for anyone.

But I was encouraging so he told me how he'd imitated a Stars Wars robot once and what a turn off that had been.

No, he hadn't tried that joke again because his date had given him a look which would have melted the insides of one of his machines...

But I was interested, really I was, and so he gave me a minute's explanation on how planning a new installation of robots was the really great part – and how satisfying it was to see all the work he had done actually in a factory producing things.

I told him about managing the kids in the call centre and trying to keep their minds off each other and on their jobs, and he seemed interested too.

We were enjoying each other's company.

*****

Simon phoned the following day, as he had promised. I was both pleased and relieved. I did fancy meeting him twice, and being dumped after just two coffees and a muffin would have been a bit of a blow.

I took the plunge. What about a meal in that new Turkish restaurant on the outskirts of town?

It wasn't a straightforward question. How to weigh the correct invitation for a second meeting? Heaven help me, I'd thought a lot about it on the way home from the coffee and muffins.

Restaurants were good because you got to sit near to your date, my God that sounded strange coming from a thirty something woman: a date!

So, yes - a restaurant where I'd be sort of near him and yet still far enough away. It wasn't like you had to sit next to your date, only near to them.

The restaurant had to be chosen carefully too. Not too posh to put him off in case he didn't normally eat at places like that but better than a curry house or café. Turkish was good. A bit exotic but not too challenging – foreign food but not stuff which was way out of the ordinary.

Simon was really polite and offered to collect me but I said no and made an excuse about needing to drop some stuff off at my friend's. This was lie – but a fair one. I didn't know him and didn't want him to see where I lived in case he turned out to be a weirdo and stalked me or something. You never knew with men these days…

I arrived on time and he was there waiting for me in the car park. We walked across to the restaurant and he held the door open for me. This was old fashioned but I liked his good manners a lot. He was a bit different from the other men I'd met recently – and a galaxy away from my ex who would have expected me to hold the door open for him!

I asked for a table near the window because I didn't want to feel trapped in a corner or an alcove. I knew he wasn't going to attack me or anything stupid like that, but being in the open made me feel safe and a little more confident.

The moment we sat down I offered to go halves on the meal. I wasn't having anything to do with this, "I'll pay for a kebab and you get your knickers off after."

I'd had to deal with that more than once since I'd got into the dating game.

But he smiled and said he'd just got a bonus for an installation which had gone extraordinarily well and this was a celebration meal.

He had an open, honest, slightly sad face so I agreed - but only if I could pay next time.

Next time? What had I said? Next time? I must be mad. What if he bored me stupid or came on hard and I didn't want a bloody next time?

What if he saw the grey streaks in my hair or thought that I wasn't clever enough or didn't like my clothes? What next time?

I ordered Köfte and he had vine leaves stuffed with currants, peppers and rice.

We shared a big plate of vegetables and a bowl of spiced rice.

I looked across at his vine leaves. "They look lovely. What's in them?"

So he told me.

"Would you like to try some?"

I hesitated momentarily and then took a fork full of the filling. As I did, the screaming in my ears was deafening. What would he think? Was I too pushy? Why did I do that?

I wanted to share his vine leaves but 'when I did' a massive number of dangerous doors opened – too much, too soon, too pushy, too slutty, too every bloody thing else!

I wished a big hole would open up and I could disappear forever.

I tried to make things better – but only made the hole deeper.

"Here, have one of my meatballs."

I moved my fork across the table, carrying a meatball balanced precariously – and then dropped it.

Bloody, bloody, bloody hell! What will he think of me?

He laughed it off, but I felt like crawling under the table.

Simon picked up the meatball and put it straight into his mouth in one go. Then he laughed. "Lovely meat ball - but I don't fancy the table cloth."

We both giggled - and I could relax.

Then he sat back and tears came into his eyes.

"What's the matter?" An avalanche of doubt and even fear swept over me.

Not again! Please bloody God, not again. What have I done now?

Simon spoke. "I'm really sorry. I really am. It was when you picked up the meat ball you looked just like Hannah."

I was genuinely confused. Hannah? Was he still in a relationship?

Two more tears rolled down his face. "It's shit! It really is and you don't deserve this.

"Hannah was my wife – and it really is a 'was'.

"She was fed up with me being away so much, so in the end she finished the marriage.

"But I miss her so much.

"And the kids.

"We've got two lovely kids.

"Do you want to see them?"

It wasn't so much a question but a statement.

I nodded.

There were hundreds of pictures of the kids on his phone - and of Hannah, who I thought was better looking than me.

And a big, floppy eared dog, jumping up for a ball in the garden.

It was like an ad for the perfect family.

Or the ad for another period of babysitting an emotional wreck.

For the next twenty minutes Simon cried and poured out his heart while I listened, in between the tears, to how much he loved Hannah and how perfect she was, how wonderful the kids were and even that Ben, the spaniel, was the best friend anyone could have.

I nodded and agreed. In my head I could see the timer running towards the moment when I would stand up and walk away.

Even so, there was sufficient time to think what a stupid, selfish cow Hannah was not to cherish a man like Simon who would have been my dream forever partner.

Now tears came into my eyes too, not of sympathy but at the intense unfairness of life. If I'd had Simon we would have had two lovely kids, and a dog, and I would have never let him go - not for anything or anyone.

But I hadn't met Simon. I'd got that bag of shit who had used my love for him for his own selfish reasons.

Now, the timer had come to an end and I had to be brave and accept the truth, however tough it was.

I knew I was full of faults as a human being and very ready to admit them, but being cruel was not one.

I spoke quite softly and with kindness.

"Simon, this isn't going to work out. I think you're lovely but you'll always have your wife and kids on your mind.

"And you should too – they look very special.

"I can't give you any marriage advice but you've got to go back to Hannah and tell her that the two of you need to make things right – for the sake of the kids, or the bloody dog or whatever: I don't know.

"But you do need to try because if you don't, you'll regret it for the rest of your life.

"Give up the posh work and get a job on the till at Tesco or somewhere.

"Just make it work."

He reached across the table and touched my hand, but I pulled it away firmly with no room for doubt: it, whatever it had been, was over.

In the car park, he held me very slightly longer, and more tightly, than platonic friendship required and then gave me a firmer kiss on my left cheek than was strictly necessary – or appropriate.

CHAPTER THREE

I was quiet the following day. I'd liked Simon a lot and there had seemed to be a real chance for something…What, I didn't know - but just anything which wasn't another failure.

Still, work always kept me occupied. Soay Customer Care – although everyone called us SCC – did a job which had to be done – but no-one wanted to do it!

Customer service is expensive and that's why when you ring up moaning about your internet not working you can end up talking – if you get through to anyone at all – to someone on the other side of the world.

SCC was the fix between a conversation with a bloke sat in a tent in the middle of the Sahara Desert and having your calls ignored altogether.

The big brands looked after their own problems so we took on the job for the stuff you find at discount prices on the internet. Everyone wants a bargain, all the time, but if you want to know why your microwave was so cheap you'll find out when you ring SCC to complain about it not working.

But it was the first step on the management ladder for me and I really, but really, wanted to do well.

Not that it was easy. I had a very young staff because crap wages and a boring job attract people who can't do any better. I knew that they talked about me behind my back – and in front of it too.

They were all totally immersed in the dating game – or, more accurately, the mating game – and I had failed at it yet again.

Emily was the worst. She so wanted to be one of the Love Island contestants – and was nearly there, but still miles away – just a tacky imitation from a pound shop.

Unfortunately, she didn't know this and I had to spend too much time reminding her of the company rules about using personal phones when she was supposed to be working and the importance of actually being at her workspace taking customers' calls.

The truth is that Emily had no interest in working on a Customer Support call line, or anywhere else for that matter. She looked, and she really did study the subject hard and endlessly, at Social Media Influencers and the vast sums of money they earned - and bitterly resented being tied to taking calls from people she considered to be whinging losers.

And the target for her frustration was always me because I was the one who made her work – or what passed for work.

Sarah - with her head stuck up her snotty arse.

Sarah - the school prefect trying to make everyone walk down the left-hand side of the corridor.

Sarah - the frigid cow who no man would look at, even if he'd not had a woman in ten years.

I tried to be empathetic but the one thing which really caused friction was the lack of interest Emily showed in customers' problems.

There was insufficient discourtesy for even a verbal warning but I got really tense when I heard a caller being fed platitudes about the problems they were facing with their washing machine, microwave or tumble drier.

Emily was at her worst with elderly or nervous callers. The moment she had finished with one there would be a mime show to the other call handlers about how well she had seen off someone who was unsure or confused or simply frightened.

So Emily led the snide comments and sniggers aimed at me – the frigid cow.

Everyone knew about them: everyone laughed, some for fear of being left out of the hunting pack and others because being cruel was satisfying, but Emily expertly steered just on the right side of being guilty of anything which might result in disciplinary action.

Sometimes - in the dulled, Netflix filled evenings after work, I was haunted by the thought that if this was all that life could offer, was it worth having at all?

*****

What hurt the most was that I did try to join in with the office culture of daytime drivel TV, clubbing – and all that went with it.

I'd really tried with the karaoke at the Christmas party and laughed when they all booed as I tried to sing 'My Heart Will Go On.'

In a quiet corner, near the stationery cupboard and very well hidden from public view, I had cried inside because the words were the ones I wanted to say to someone…

When they sprayed me with Prosecco as a prize for the worst song of the night I stood on a chair, laughed and waved the bottle over my head like some Formula One Champion.

Thank God I had enough soberness still left in me not to spray the computers with cheap Italian bubbly or I would have been playing cards with the General Manager the following day – and mine would have been a P45!

I'd even let Josh stare at my wet shirt, which was showing my bra very clearly underneath, but I gave him a warning glare when he said that we should have a wet t-shirt competition for the next Christmas Party.

Bloody hell! There I was: an intelligent woman trying her best in life having to suffer the indignity of having a teenage kid stare at her breasts.

And for what?

*****

The day after the Christmas party something unusual happened and, strangely, it made me feel much better.

I didn't have a proper office, with a door which closed, but I did have a sort of big cubicle, glass walled on three sides and with a table and a few plastic chairs where I could sit down and discuss any changes to what we were able to offer angry customers – which was never anything above the bare legal minimum.

It was also where I had to listen to a soft sob story about a funeral that one of them had to attend, or a dental appointment or some such crap, just to avoid work.

There was an unwritten, but very clear, rule that when there was only one of them talking to me at the table, no-one else would interrupt us because it was considered "private."

Josh – the near baby who had been staring at my boobs the previous night - hesitated outside and made the faintest attempt at knocking on the glass wall.

"Have you got a minute?" He smiled a weak, teenage smile.

"Yes of course Josh? What's up?"

He almost shuffled in, like coming to the teacher's desk and I waved my hand towards a chair and smiled. I didn't know what the problem would be but whatever it was I would do my best to help because I couldn't be a ruthless bastard no matter how hard I tried.

Josh fidgeted with his phone, like some baby with a comfort toy, and then said, "Well, you know last night when you got sprayed with Prosecco?"

He hesitated, and I forced a smile, "Well – well, it was wrong. They went too far and it wasn't fair and I want you to know that it wasn't fair.

I smiled – just slightly – and said, "Thanks Josh. That's very kind but Christmas parties always get a bit rowdy and it was all just a bit of fun…"

And inside me the enormity of the lie I had just told to Josh, and myself, burnt like a raging fire.

"And there's another thing. I looked at your boobs and I thought that they were great but I shouldn't have stared.

"Mike from accounts had brought some weed in and I don't

normally do this but it was Christmas and the booze and I'd never been to an office Christmas Party before and I didn't want everyone saying that I was a dick and should still be at school – you know how it is…

"But staring at you like that was well out of order and I'm sorry I did, but you really are gorgeous…

"And I'm sorry if I shouldn't have said that either."

He fiddled with his comfort phone again.

"If you ever fancied a drink or something…?"

I seemed to have spent all my life being kind to bloody blokes, and children now. I could have slapped him down but knew I never would.

Josh was a fit young man and, of all the staff on the floor, the nicest and the most willing to help customers.

There was another thing too. I looked at his shirt, tight across his chest, and I knew that there would be plenty more worth seeing.

So, the big question roaring across my mind was did I want sex with a fit, pleasant teenager? Was it enough to have nice young man fancy me?

It wasn't a difficult question. I hadn't gone off sex, but it seemed so long ago that I'd probably have to check Wikipedia to remember how to do it. I wanted more than just laying on my back for a couple of minutes and then washing myself down in the bathroom.

I wanted a man who had lived – someone I could talk to, who'd been bashed by life like me, who would cradle my head and gently stroke my hair and tell me that he loved me – and then we'd be one.

Josh could never give me any of this – and it would be wrong to expect him to be able to.

I said, "Thanks Josh, but I've got so much on at the moment that I barely have a spare moment for even a coffee.

"But I do appreciate the offer, I really do. That was very kind."

And I shuffled some papers to let him know that it was time for him to go.

*****

What Josh had said made me feel a lot better but as for the rest of team – and the word team was a joke – it was as bad as ever.

As always, Love Island Emily needed to feed on the fact that I wasn't her and never would be. She was never content to be passive, or even neutral, but needed to attack me and what she called 'my sort' simply to survive – like some virus which has to eat its host in order to thrive.

A few weeks later I was in a cubicle in the female toilets when I heard Emily and Julia come in giggling.

"I bloody hate that stuck up cow," Emily said, "she's always on at me."

"Her problem is that she's not had a shag for years."

Julia joined in. "Yeah, you can just imagine it.

"Get your pants off and I'm going to time how long it takes you to come.

"And I want you to thank me at the end.

"And tidy up afterwards so that we look professional."

"If you sent her a gift card she'd send it back saying it was the wrong colour."

Both girls laughed hysterically.

Outside the door I could hear them laughing – at me, for not being one of them.

Inside the cubicle, I fought back the tears and anger.

To be honest, it was a long time before I had the courage to return to the call centre floor.

CHAPTER FOUR

That night, I simply could not face opening "More Than Friends" so I channel surfed until I came across a programme describing the life of the Giant River Otter in South America.

The film showed Mrs Otter getting the full hit attention from Mr Otter and I wondered what it would be like to be really wanted – really cared for and at the centre of someone's life, even a 2m long otter!

The only fix was going to be my bestie, the artisan gin bottle – hand-made happiness wrapped in glass. In goes the sparkling tonic, inviting me to the party, and on goes the gin - and there's my escape from the sadness: easy.

My phone bonged pleasantly telling me that a message had arrived. It was almost a mass mailing except that I knew the woman who had sent it very well. It was Polly Tatton. Tiny, slim, very pretty Polly who had every lad in our Grad year begging for her attention but was more interested, vastly more interested, in protecting urban wildlife.

Ten years later Polly had become nationally known through her Social Media videos and podcasts.

Our relationship was a strange one. Polly used to sit in my room at Uni for hours talking about nothing, drinking my coffee, eating my biscuits – and sharing the Chardonnay she sometimes brought for us.

More than once, I had removed Polly's shoes and covered her up with the throw from the settee. Then I would tiptoe across the room to bed – knowing that she'd still be asleep when the alarm went off the following morning: we were that close.

My room was a chill out space for Polly – away from the constant attention of the opposite sex, no need to be careful about the next word she said and free from the evangelism she practised.

Now, Polly was to be found circulating on the media circus in London but she had come to Kinton for a special reason - and that was the internationally famous, wildlife photographer Mick Hargrave who just happened to be a local man.

Now she was inviting me to the Kinton Gallery of Modern Art where, somehow, she'd persuaded Mick to bring some of his finest urban wildlife images for a one night exhibition.

There was a champagne reception sponsored by La Table Française, the go-to eatery for the local posh people, and afterwards an auction of signed prints.

All very, very posh but Polly would be so happy to see me again – would I come please? Please, please?

I hesitated, poured the gin and tonic crutch, and then replied.

"Hey Polly, that's so kind and I really don't deserve the invite. But I'd love to come.

"Lots of love

"XXXXX"

A reply came almost instantly.

"It'll be sooo good to see you again. I still miss our Chardonnay nights 😊

"I heard that things didn't work out with you and Brandon and you never know your luck at one of these shows.

"Fingers crossed!"

*****

I went into my bedroom, opened the wardrobe doors and pulled back the clothes rail.

Right at the back, well hidden from view, was a white and black dress bag. I kept it well out of sight for fear of remembering what was in it.

Inside, perched neatly on a velvet hanger, was my black silk dress with its fitted bodice, uncompromising waist and almost non-existent shoulder straps, each one with a tiny silver butterfly at the front.

Beneath the dress, in their box, were the black, patent leather, strappy stiletto sandals which went with it – beautiful, impractical things with tiny heels and so different from the sensible trainers I wore to work.

I ran my hand down the glass-smooth heel of the shoe and remembered how utterly feminine I had felt wearing them.

As my fingers grazed the smooth fabric of the dress, memories of laughter, confidence, and whispered promises resurfaced. The contrast between my life now and the vibrant, carefree person I once was, stung.

In another box was the gold necklace which my Gran had bequeathed to me, wonderfully worn but so full of love.

I picked it up and it was cool to my touch, as if it had been neglected. The necklace needed to come out into the light and be seen, admired and loved again.

There was another box next to the necklace and I knew what was in it. I was never lavish, and spent little on luxuries, but the silver bangle had screamed out to me from the window of the antique shop.

It wasn't a big clunky thing but nor was it thin and delicate. The shop owner said that it had been made in Birmingham in 1928 and it was in amazingly good condition for its age, with all the engraving sharp and clear.

And that engraving was what made it so special. On it was just the one word: Sarah – some other Sarah from the previous century had put the bangle on her wrist and I smiled because she had thought it beautiful once – just as I did now. It was beautiful and I felt wonderful wearing it.

So I got out my credit card and £45 later I became the second Sarah in the bracelet's life.

I wore it all that evening and it was a magical experience when the silver warmed with my body heat so that it became part of me – Sarah's silver bracelet: two of us, both Sarahs.

When I showed it to Brandon his only question was a near grunted, "What'd cost?"

I could have slapped him, "Less than you spend in the bloody pub on a Sunday!"

Hurt by Brandon's reaction to the bracelet, I hid it away and, even when we went to parties, I never wore it again.

Now I would. I'd wear the tight dress and shiny shoes, Gran's necklace and the silver bracelet – my silver bracelet, just as the first Sarah had worn it all those years ago.

There was more. Hiding almost shyly was the bottle of Chanel Coco that my dad had bought for me when I got my degree.

This was going to be the first step to great things. Dad always wanted the best for me so somehow he'd found £85 and said that I should wear the Chanel every day for work.

Unfortunately for him, and me, making sandwiches on the production line at Berwick's Bakery was not the place to be wearing Chanel!

But there was still some left. Just a tiny dab on each wrist, another on my neck and, most importantly of all, between my boobs, would be enough to show that I deserved to be at Urban Animals and Us.

Then I stood back, looked in the mirror and knew that it was never going to happen – not without some drastic and instant action.

*****

The longest journey needs the first step – and three and a bit weeks was not going to be a long journey!

I almost marched back into the living room and saw the bottle of gin smiling encouragingly at me. It was already past G&T-

o'clock and my body was reminding me that it wanted a drink – and unambiguously too.

8pm. Gin, tonic and Netflix. Those were the rules. And don't forget the bonus size bag of tortilla chips either!

Now the rules had changed. I picked up the half bottle of gin, looked at it accusingly, and then put it right at the very back of the wall unit where it was going to stay!

The tortilla chips went too. The black dress hovered in front of my eyes like a motorway warning sign.

"Danger," it said. "Lose weight now or you'll never get into me."

Instead of "More Than Friends" I hit the dieting web sites hard – really hard!

With the sort of dieting I had in mind there were warnings everywhere about taking advice from professionals and being sensible and all the mainstream stuff - but the black dress was sending a different message.

For the next two hours, and only with cups of coffee for a crutch, I checked out the diet plans – how to do the job properly and lose a guaranteed two pounds in weight every week.

And there were all the smiling faces, nearly all women by the way, showing how they'd lost a stone in six months.

Bloody hell! That's all very interesting but I need to lose a whole dress size in three weeks. This wasn't the time to be sensible and sit round in a group with a load of other women giving each other badges for not having an Eccles cake with their coffee on a single morning.

Then I came across a site with a big monster munching its way across the screen, screaming "I'm the Fat Eater."

The plan was called, "When the Going Gets Tough – Dieting for People Who Really Want to Lose Weight Fast."

So I entered my details, with a fake name and an e-mail address I hardly ever use, paid my £19.99 and got a diet plan back immediately, along with a load of tips about staying healthy on what was going to be a tough journey.

I almost wished that I hadn't.

To be fair to the site, there were a range of choices. To be fair to me, none of them were what I wanted to eat.

I ticked the boxes for the first day, wrinkled my nose at the screen and balled my fists. I was going to get into my black dress and I was going to the exhibition looking lovely.

Breakfast
Oatmeal with fruit and nuts (250 calories)

Lunch
Small Tuna salad sandwich on whole-grain bread with carrot sticks (420 calories)

Dinner
Grilled salmon with roasted vegetables and brown rice (500 calories)

Snacks
Protein smoothie with Greek yogurt and spinach (200 calories)

Beverages
Water (aim for 8-10 glasses/day)
Black coffee

Tips
1. Eat five meals/day (three main, two snacks)
2. Control portion sizes
3. Avoid processed foods, sugary drinks, and saturated fats
4. Incorporate physical activity (cardio, strength training)
5. Monitor progress, adjust calorie intake accordingly

"Suffer" factor:
1. Reduce sugar intake drastically
2. Incorporate intermittent fasting (12-14 hours/day)
3. Increase physical activity intensity

It was going to be hard, but you know what? I wasn't put off – not a bit. I knew in my heart that I was worth more than being asked out by a teenager whose only interest was seeing me flat on my back with my legs in the air, or becoming a free psychiatric counsellor for some bloke who'd gone through a terrible divorce. I was definitely worth more than this – and the start was the little black dress.

I went to bed hungry – and with the siren voice of the gin bottle shouting loudly at me through the wall unit door.

This was going to be a toughie.

*****

I slept badly but got up fizzing with enthusiasm because I was doing something for me.

I didn't even do the plan properly. Breakfast was a cup of black coffee with two sweeteners. It was a stupid way to go about a diet but before I left for work I unzipped the secret bag again and looked at the black dress. Its message was clear. Lose a complete dress size - or you and me will never see each other.

When I had a bottle of still water on my desk, instead of the non-stop cups of coffee, the office gossip began: Sarah was dieting – with all that meant. That's how quickly the word spread.

Ste went to get some croissants and brownies. He wasn't in my team but he was the most polite of all the floor workers and always offered to get something for me. My go to fat-and-sugar fix was a cinnamon roll – now it wasn't. I could see the 500 calories actually hovering in front of me like some alien message.

"Eat a cinnamon roll and split your black dress."

So I said, "Thanks Ste, but I'm not hungry this morning." All round the office there were knowing looks…

By lunch-time I felt as if there was a large capybara gnawing away inside me.

I used to enjoy watching these giant rats at Chester Zoo and now a massive one had made its burrow inside me and its great yellow teeth were intent on chewing right through my stomach.

At lunch-time, I headed straight into town. There were two reasons. Exercise was going to help shed a few calories but I had a check list too. Brown rice, whole grain pasta, hummus and herbal teas. For sure, it was going to be a different way of living.

The only mistake that I made was walking down the snack isle to reach the pasta. A thousand packets of tortilla chips, nachos and crisps all reached out at me like some horror movie.

"Eat us and feel better!" they screamed in unison - but I didn't.

What I did do was stick to the diet rigidly, I mean hard core. When Ste brought the croissants round in the morning I didn't even smell them, let alone actually eat one and at the end of the week the scales spoke to me: three whole pounds gone and still two and a half weeks left.

As well as watching every calorie, and I really did get to know each one individually by name, I hit the exercise hard too. I was never a great athlete at school but I was always fit and before Brandon banned us from skiing, I was pretty good.

So, straight after my tea – if you can call it that – I put my sweatshirt on and set off to speed walk, first for half an hour and then a bit longer and faster every night.

I would be lying if I said that I was enjoying what I was doing but I did feel better in myself – and the artisan gin bottle never moved a millimetre from the wall unit. Eventually, it dozed off and stopped calling me.

At the end of the second week I nearly shouted out with joy –

yes, proper delight. Seven pounds had gone now. Seven whole bloody pounds. How good was that!

For a treat, I took out the black dress and held it up against me. The dress smiled encouragingly and said, in dress speak that only women can understand, "You can't quite get into me but give it another week..."

Then one of its little silver butterflies winked encouragingly at me.

The sandals slid on too as if they were made for me. You know, this dieting wasn't too bad.

I waited until the end of week three before weighing myself for the last time.

And I had to sit down on the edge of the bed I was so pleased – and proud too. I'd lost seven pounds. That's nearly a whole dress size. So, stick that up your bums Emily and Julia.

I couldn't stop myself from crying.

I said a silent prayer and then went to the wardrobe and took out the black silk dress – my dress.

It was a tiny bit tight but I still had four days to go and I was in it. Completely and totally inside my dress and without the seams bursting. It was wonderful.

The following day, after work, I went to Delamere Dreams in Chester to finish off the job. I wanted seamless black knickers and a really pretty bra so that I looked like the woman I felt inside – not someone who spent all day rounding up teenage cats in a call centre or answering messages from men who I wouldn't be seen dead with, but me – Sarah Bersham. Okay, not a Leonardo di Caprio supermodel but a decent looking woman with nice clothes and a brain.

It was quiet in the shop and the lady on the fitting room desk had a lovely smile and time to talk. I showed her my black dress, so that she didn't think that I'd been shoplifting or something, and the black knickers and bra I wanted to try on. This was a serious job and I just had to get everything right.

The knickers were pretty standard seamless jobs but the black bra was absolutely stunning – not padded because I didn't need any help in this department but with a bit of lift so that what I had naturally looked at its best. The top half was a lovely lace filigree and it looked worth every penny of the £39 price tag.

I was so pleased, so completely satisfied that I could fit into the 34B perfectly - just as I used to do.

The knickers were just what they said on the packet and so I slipped into the little black dress and had a long look in the mirror.

I'm not given to girlie squealing but if I ever was, this was the time because I thought I looked lovely.

I pulled the curtain in the fitting room back a little bit and did a mini twirl for the lady at the desk. "What do you think?"

She was silver haired and looked like the Fairy Godmother from the panto at Runcorn. She beamed and said, "Oh, you look great. I wish I still had a figure like yours."

And she smiled so encouragingly that my credit card didn't even feel the pain.

It did two days later though. Easter Bonnet was not my sort of hairdresser, not by a long way, but I thought of all the money I had saved by not having croissants and treated myself to everything they had on offer – the full works.

And I did feel better for it.

At last, I was me – not some TikTok imitation with false bits stuck on everywhere but me, in my lovely black dress and my gran's gold necklace and with Sarah's lovely silver bracelet on my left wrist.

I was going to show them all who I really was.

CHAPTER FIVE

Polly sent me a lot of WhatsApp messages. She told me how the old engineering works which had been transformed into the Kinton Gallery of Modern Art was being given a real makeover and how having Mick Hargrave show his pictures there really was a big deal – especially for a small gallery.

Then she mentioned that there would be a lot of men there. Not men but M-E-N and who knows what I might take home with me as a souvenir of the evening?

With anyone else, I would have thought that this was a bit pushy but with Polly it was different. She'd never liked Brandon and had been delighted when he'd gone.

Now, she wanted to do some discreet – or knowing Polly, a bit less than discreet – match making.

I thought of the little black dress and smiled, grateful that Polly was on my side.

*****

There was no shortage of charity shops wherever I went. In the end, I found exactly what I was looking for in a shop raising money for spinal injuries. In their window was a grey and black faux fur jacket which looked brand-new. That's a lie! It was better than brand-new, still with its Sosandar carry bag. It looked as if it had never even been tried on. I was almost embarrassed – but not very, because of how much money I was spending on everything else - to hand over £35.

Now, my mission was complete – I had my little black dress and all the things which went with it; a brand-new jacket, my jewellery and Chanel perfume.

I could be the real thing.

*****

That night, I got dressed for battle, right down to the last detail. I looked in the wardrobe mirror and smiled: I was a bit more than okay.

I took a selfie – two actually, one with just the black dress and the other with the dress and Sosandar jacket – and then I sent them to Polly.

I got a reply almost instantly.

"Wow! OMG you look amazing! I know someone who will really want to meet you!" And she finished with ✨ and 💃

*****

As we exchanged more texts, I sensed that there was a change in how Polly was thinking about me.

She was very kind and that's why she'd invited me: a mate from a previous life. But now things were shifting – and quite quickly too.

Before the exhibition opened there was a private, VIP reception for VIP guests – and I was invited. How good was that?

Polly said that the champagne would be flowing and to make sure that I came by taxi.

*****

The Uber driver arrived early but I was already waiting – completely ready for the evening ahead. I hadn't been to many receptions, and certainly not any VIP ones, but somehow I felt relaxed and confident. All the small parts had come together – the little black dress, posh underwear, the Chanel, Gran's necklace and my Sarah bracelet: I felt complete.

When I got to the gallery there were a couple of posh bouncers on the door. OMG! This was the real thing! The exhibition was through the main doors, in the large area where parts used to be finished in the old days of engineering, and the reception was off to one side.

The bouncer actually said, "This way please, Madam."

Bloody, bloody, bloody hell! He called me Madam and said please. I glowed inside. Clearly, the black dress was working its magic.

I'm not sure whether it was a lady bouncer, or just a receptionist who spent a lot of time in the gym, but my coat was taken and there I was – in a large room, elegantly laid out with immaculate tables set with embroidered white tablecloths and beautiful China plates loaded with all sort of nibbles – and buckets and buckets full of Champagne bottles.

Polly floated across and she looked the business too - in a beige trouser suit which showed off her ash blonde hair perfectly.

Her hug was genuinely warm and enthusiastic.

"Soooo lovely to see you. Oh wow! You look better in real life than the selfies – and you looked fantastic in them!

"Come and meet some people."

And off we went…

"Luke, this is my dear friend from Uni, Sarah Bersham. She works in management."

I nearly blushed with gratitude when I thought what management actually meant – getting wannabee Influencers to leave TikTok alone and do some work.

"Luke has developed the app which allows us to keep track of urban wildlife so that everyone can see how we're doing in protecting the animals who share our world with us."

That sounded just like the other Polly: the evangelist who had led protest marches about the urbanisation of the environment, even in her first year at Uni.

I smiled at Luke but barely got a flicker of acknowledgement back from him. Where everyone else was in suits he wore faded, tan coloured chinos and an equally worn out t-shirt carrying a picture of an angry looking hawk. A tired denim jacket finished the outfit.

He had his phone in one hand, and the moment Polly had stopped speaking he was looking at it furtively, no doubt expecting a text or WhatsApp message from President Trump or the Nobel Prize Committee or something because he was clearly a very, very important person.

But I was determined that nothing was going to spoil my evening – nothing and no-one.

I said, "It must be fascinating to be able to make something which is really helping us understand wildlife."

He looked up from his phone. "Yeah, I decided as a kid that I didn't want to waste my time just going through the motions of living a life (and I couldn't stop myself from thinking about the call centre) and Apps were the doors to the new world where we're all going to be living soon."

And he looked back at his phone again.

Like I said, I'm always the trier so I said, "That's an impressive looking kestrel on your shirt, like the ones they used to use for hunting." And that I added my best interested smile.

This time, he did make eye contact. "It's a Sparrow Hawk – not a kestrel. They're being forced into urban environments because there are too many humans polluting the planet."

Then he began texting someone so I guessed that my job interview was well and truly over and I'd better move on.

This was easy though, even without Polly making any introductions. An immaculate waiter – and he was worth looking at until I saw the wedding ring – floated towards me with a silver tray of drinks.

"Would Madam like champagne?"

Well, Madam most certainly would because Madam was more than a bit fond of Le Bubbly and Madam did know the difference between Le Real Thing and La Discountio Prosecco – so there, Mr App Man!

There were plates of canapés – I think that this is what they were although I am not really up to speed with VIP food – so I helped myself to an exquisite little tart filled with cream cheese and a sliver of smoked salmon on top.

Thank goodness I'd not got into the champagne properly because after the diet I'd have had the whole tray – and the little biscuity things with roasted tomatoes on top and some tiny slices of pizza and...

Just then Polly floated back into view with a smile which would have melted an iceberg, not that she would ever melt any icebergs because of the polar bears and penguins and things.

You can see that the champers was starting to loosen me up!

"Come and say hello to Mr and Mrs Kumar. If you've bought any petrol for miles around, it will be from one of Mr and Mrs Kumar's stations." And she beamed.

Even if you didn't have the slightest bit of interest in urban wildlife when you began talking to Polly you'd be a fan after two minutes – she is genuinely charismatic.

Mr Kumar was immaculate in a dark blue suit but Mrs Kumar was take-your-breath-away-stunning, in the most beautiful red and gold sari.

It was so feminine with her right shoulder showing a gold embroidered Indian blouse. Then there was a tiny sliver of her waist visible. Wow!

I couldn't help myself. "You look incredible – absolutely amazing." And I beamed a full on fan smile.

Mrs Kumar, dipped her head ever so slightly and smiled. "Thank you – but I'm not the only one with a nice dress. You look absolutely beautiful."

All that I could manage was a rather limp, "Thank you."

It was really a bit odd but when she made the comment, I became hugely more relaxed. I felt that I should be here. My parents had made sure that I was well brought up within what they could afford and I'd done well at school and Uni.

It was men who were my weak point. I just seemed to have permanent bad luck...

Mr Kumar turned to me. "Look, we know your name but we've been so bad mannered.

"I'm Vivek and this is my wife Hiranmayi.

They were genuinely charming – utterly lovely people.

I said, "I'm so pleased to meet you..." And I was.

"Polly said that you own lots of filling stations?" I felt slightly out of my comfort zone because I wasn't sure whether you called them garages or filling stations or petrol shops or something really technical.

It was Hiranmayi who answered, with a real grin. "Yes, we have fifteen of them now.

"Vivek's dad began the business and we've worked hard to grow it.

"Tell Sarah the story, Vivek, you tell stories much better than me."

"It wasn't complicated. We lived in Uganda and were Ugandans through and through. General Idi Amin had a dream and God told him that all Asians were bad for Uganda and so we were all kicked out in 1972.

"90 days to get out and that was that. We were homeless and penniless."

It all seemed so bloody unfair. To lose everything because someone had a mad dream from God.

"Go on Vivek."

He nodded. "We arrived in London but Dad heard that there was more work in the north so we borrowed the money for the train fare and ended up here.

"He was a highly skilled engineer – the real deal – but no-one wanted him. So, he got a job as a cleaner in a garage which sold petrol on the side.

"He used to tell me that he loved even getting the toilet bowls gleaming – he just wanted everything perfect.

"When the owner retired, my dad scraped all the money he could from anywhere and got a bank loan. And that was the start.

"Fifteen filling stations later, that's where we are now."

And he smiled. "We owe a lot to this country."

"But what about you?"

So I told them, about the men failures – highlights only of course – and how now I spent my days rounding up teenage cats in the call centre and trying to get them to do their jobs properly.

"The biggest problem that I have is than no-one in management is even a bit interested in the level of service we give.

"The staff are only paid a few pence an hour above minimum wage. They don't want to be there and boy do they show it!

"I've tried to do some things like having a little prize for the best worker that month – I even bought a bottle of wine out of my own money – but my manager put a stop to the idea: he said it'd just cause trouble.

"So, I do the best that I can but it's no fun."

Vivek looked at Hiranmayi and she gave a barely imperceptible nod – really almost impossible to see.

"We've got 134 staff – I think it is 134 because the number changes every day – and I'm always looking for good managers who can motivate them.

"There'd be a car too – and we would be interested in you getting the best from our staff.

"Here's my card – have a think if you fancy a career change."

I was thinking. If this is what the little black dress was doing for me I was going to wear it every day – and sleep in it too!

To actually be offered a job, a proper job with prospects and a car took my breath away. Yes, I was Sarah Bersham and yes, I was worth something and yes, loads of other good things as well. The thoughts swept through me like some super drug.

But before I could say anything more to the Kumars, Polly floated into view again – this time actually holding on to the sleeve of a man.

Straight away I thought that he had never tried to make an

impression in his life because he was born impressive! Early 40s. Black hair with a few grey streaks. Fashionably designer stubble. Immaculate dinner suit. Brilliant white shirt with so, so classy gold cuff links.

Polly beamed. "This Florian Montignac. Florian owns La Table Française who are sponsoring tonight's exhibition.

"Florian wanted to say hello…"

The Kumars just gently disappeared along with Polly, without actually leaving, and Florian gave me a little bow – honestly he did, and held out his hand.

"Hello Sarah. I'm delighted to meet you. Polly has told me all about the fun you two had together at University."

I managed a smile, "Yes, we were very close although she's gone on to be a superstar and I haven't…"

This time it took some real effort to squeeze out anything which even vaguely resembled a smile.

"And you own La Table Française? I've always wanted to eat there but it's a bit out of my price bracket. I'm more your Indian or Maccy Ds."

"That's very funny. I'm sure that your tastes are much more refined than that but it would be my pleasure to have you as my guest one evening."

And he reached into his pocket and gave me a business card – oak brown with embossed black writing. Talk about classy!

"Give my PA a ring and she'll arrange it all and, if I can, I'll be there too."

I sort of mumbled "Thanks" and without trying he somehow caught the attention of the waiter, the dishy one who now looked definitely second division, and swept a glass of champagne off the tray and gave it to me.

"It's not the very best but my family owns a share in one of the smaller Champagne houses so I like to keep the business in the family."

Like you do. Yes, my mum and dad make champagne too. Doesn't everyone?

He nodded towards the exhibition and said, "Shall we?"

He held out his arm for me to rest my hand on. I felt just like a princess or a film star walking into the show with royalty.

Florian was really good company – knowledgeable, interested in me, funny and so different from the men I had met in the past.

I also noticed that he was interested in a bit more than the prints and my company. The little black dress was very modest but showed enough to let any man know what was there – and Florian was very interested.

I was glad that I'd invested in the seamless knickers too!

The wildlife prints were stunning. It was amazing to think that there were so many animals we never think of as living in towns, right there alongside us.

It was one of the best evenings of my life. I felt like me – how I should have been all these years. I was with a gorgeous man and he fancied me, I could tell that without a shadow of a doubt, and it felt great. Not some selfish bastard using me as a cook, housekeeper and psychiatrist nor a drooling teenager staring at my boobs but a real man, a classy man who saw me and liked what he saw.

The talk given by Mick Hargrave was brilliant. Everyone clapped and, by this time, Florian was standing very close to me – sort of, "You wear expensive aftershave, don't you?" close.

Polly came across as people were starting to leave and said, with a very knowing smile, "You two seem to be getting on very well so I'll say goodnight – and hope that you have a lovely rest of the evening."

Florian looked at me – and I looked at him.

Then he said, "Would you like a digestif at my place, and then my driver can you run you home?

"It'll be much more civilised than a taxi" – and there was that confident smile.

Florian magicked another glass of champagne for me and then we went to get my coat. Thank heaven I hadn't got it from the "Any Offers" rack at the charity shop!

Florian held my coat up, for me to slip into. This was utterly amazing. I felt like a real lady – and I loved it.

Then he held the door open for me and we went into the lobby.

In no time at all, a big black Mercedes pulled up and Florian opened the door for me again – I was really starting to like this – and off we purred.

Florian sat close to me but not that sort of close. He had his arm behind me, near but not actually touching. I was Champagne happy. He'd been wonderful company and I felt so good.

Had I not been in such a relaxed place then maybe I'd have noticed what happened next – or perhaps not.

The driver said, "Will you be needing me later, sir?"

"No that's fine Jason. You get off home."

Now what did that mean? After a night of being treated like a princess and plenty of champagne, it didn't mean anything – not a single thing.

Florian's house was a massive, mock Tudor property on what was called, by people like me, millionaire's row on Wervine Lane. Every house on Wervine Lane was huge and very expensive.

The lights were on inside. Florian opened the front door, cancelled the alarm and said, "Welcome to my home – at least, my home when I am in England."

It had an odd feel to it. You notice these things as a woman. It was more than immaculate. I'm sure that if there had been a speck of dust anywhere it would have been polished, but it felt as if no-one really lived there – like a film set or something.

The other thing which I noticed, only for a moment, was the way Florian looked at me. I'll be honest: I desperately wanted him to look and fancy me. But this was just on the wrong side of things. Not actually leering but assessing my boobs, my bum and maybe even my face and hair – but probably not my face and hair when I look back.

Florian guided me through to a massive lounge with a TV about the size of my kitchen table and a drinks' cabinet which filled a whole wall.

He asked, "Now, what can I get for you?

He paused, "I have a friend who makes some excellent Chardonnay in Meursault. Would you like to try a glass?"

Of course, had Florian said, "I've got this glass of gnat's wee do you fancy that?" I'd have said yes.

This was an evening to remember.

Florian brought the drink to me but put it down on the large glass coffee table.

Then he kissed me – on the lips, and hard too.

"You're very attractive. You stood out tonight and I just had to get to know you better."

What could I think but wow!? Here's me, an Assistant Manager in a call centre, who blunders round from one loser bloke to another, and now a millionaire restaurant owner tells me I'm gorgeous.

Bloody hell! I owe the little black dress a present.

He kissed me again – but harder still, and this time it felt uncomfortable. Of course, I wanted to be kissed by Florian. In fact, I might well have wanted a lot more than just being kissed on the lips – but not like this.

He put his hand behind my back and pulled me close to him. I could feel that bit of him hard against me and I'm sure he knew this.

I wanted to try to take the tension out of situation so I wriggled out of his way, picked up the glass of Chardonnay and took a sip.

"Your pal can certainly make outstanding wine…" and I smiled trying to make things right between us again.

"Yes, he's one of the best.

"I'll be back in a moment. I just need to get out of this dinner jacket and into something more comfortable."

Like I said before, everything was perfect — the pictures on the wall, a little bronze statue of a girl ballet dancer, it was all too right. I wondered how much time Florian actually spent here.

I didn't have to wait long for Florian to return — bare footed and wearing just a pair of small black boxer shorts which showed everything. He paused for a second to just make sure I saw.

He grabbed me and his hands were everywhere — just groping, with no affection or care.

"No, don't Florian."

But he just kissed me even harder. He put his hand into the back of my dress and pulled me really tight against him and I knew what he wanted to do next.

"Florian! Don't! You're hurting me."

But he pushed his hands down my knickers and started squeezing my bum, forcing me closer.

I was furious, screaming, blazing angry - and upset too.

"Get off! Get off me now! What the bloody hell do you think you're doing?"

I pushed him away with all my strength and I felt the back of my dress tear.

He was still holding my left wrist and so I pushed him again. His finger caught in the clasp of my Sarah bracelet and it fell to the ground.

"You bastard! What gives you the bloody right to think that you can treat me like this?"

He laughed — he actually laughed at me.

"What do you think I brought you here for? A game of Candy Crush?"

I was crying, not big tears like when your Nanna dies, but tears of incensed anger at what he had done, and the unfairness of it all.

He went to the drinks' cabinet and picked up his wallet. He took out two £20 notes and threw them at me.

"Here. Fuck off and get yourself a taxi."

I just lost it and launched myself at him. "You arrogant, stuck up bastard! If you were the last man on the planet I wouldn't let a piece of shit like you near me!

"You might be rich but you're nothing – and you'll never be rich enough to buy me - not with all your champagne and cars.

"You're nothing."

And I got down on my hands and knees and picked up my bracelet. My Sarah bracelet. I was Sarah and I couldn't be bought by him or anyone else.

*****

It was pouring down outside – an absolute monsoon. I'd left the faux fur jacket in his house and I wasn't going back for it – not for anything – so I walked down Wervine Lane with my hair plastered to my face and my little black dress sticking to me like a swimsuit.

The rain was so heavy that it actually stung my face and I was glad. I wanted it to hurt, to wipe out what I was feeling inside – rejected, worthless in his eyes except for a one night stand and all my efforts to be me had failed.

A cab drew up alongside me. The driver dropped his window. "You okay love?

"You can't be walking out in this weather."

He paused but I couldn't say anything. The kindness was too much. Here I was, soaked, shivering and obviously on life's scrap heap and yet someone had stopped to be kind just because I needed help.

It was so far away from the dirty, selfish bastard that was Florian I couldn't stop myself from crying.

The tears rolled down my wet cheeks and I wiped them away with the back of my hand. For half a moment, I wanted the little hankie my mum used to make me take to school every day.

"Look, I can't let you pay for the cab: I'd lose my licence in a flash if I did. But you look a real mess. How about I give you a lift home for free – and don't offer me a penny or I'm dead."

All that I could say was "Thanks."

I got in and tried not to wet his seat too much as my black dress squelched under me.

On the way home I tried to hide my tears but I could see the driver having quick looks at me in his mirror, checking that I was okay.

When we pulled up outside my house I said, "Look, please let me give you something – no-one will know."

He smiled gently and said, "No. You've given me all I need just knowing you're home safe.

"My daughter's your age and if a cabbie had seen her in the mess you're in, I hope he'd have stopped to help her.

"Get yourself in and warm and dry.

"That's all I need to know."

I couldn't help myself for what happened next. I got out of the cab, went to the front door and opened it. Then I gave the driver a kiss on the cheek and a little hug. I know that wasn't very 2025 but I just had to do it.

He smiled again. "Thanks love. You paid the full fare – and I've got a tip too.

"I don't know what happened but whatever it was will be a bit better tomorrow so just you look after yourself."

I wiped away some more tears and nodded at him. "I will."

"Now, I've got to go and earn some money.

And he closed his door and drove off.

*****

I went straight to the bathroom and ran the shower. As it was warming I looked at my little black dress, sodden, torn and shapeless on the floor.

I looked in the mirror at me too. What was so bad that I couldn't find a man to like me, to fancy me and want to love to me as much as I loved him? What was the problem?

Then I stood in the shower and washed and washed myself until there wasn't a trace of Chanel on me – or anything of that bastard Florian either.

I lifted my face to the shower and let the tears run down my face, down my whole body and did nothing to stop them.

Eventually, I had nothing left so I dried myself off, put on my dressing gown and got out the gin. The wall clock said ten past two in the morning but I didn't care. The crystal clear, non-judgemental gin was my best friend again.

CHAPTER SIX

I had already booked the following day off work so I was still in bed when my phone buzzed on my bedside table. Bloody hell! It said 10.17. The last time I'd been asleep this late was on a flight back from Disney World in America.

It was Polly.

She was so bubbly and enthusiastic that I thought she'd found some new drug and had taken a double dose.

"Hiya, Star of the Show. Oooohhh - go on, do tell! How did the rest of the evening go?"

There was too long a pause and Polly, always finely tuned to what was happening around her, said, "You okay?"

I still hesitated. The truth was that, even with the heavy dose of gin, I'd not slept all night. There had been so many questions torturing me.

What did I expect after hitting the champagne so hard and letting a millionaire give me the VIP treatment?

When I saw him looking at me at the show, I knew what was on his mind. I wasn't some twelve year old at a Christmas party. I'd just told lies to myself that he really was interested in me because I wanted him to be.

And at his house...

He wasn't looking at my bra because he was passionate about lingerie design.

Like he said, what did I expect, a game of Candy Crush?

Was it all my fault?

Would I have slept with him? Would I? A good looking millionaire, with a giant house and a chauffeur?

And me - starry eyed and filled with his champagne?

As the sky got lighter through my bedroom window - I knew the answer.

No! I wouldn't have been in his bed because he was covered in big shouty labels saying, "Look at me – I'm a superstar!"

But if he had been kind, shown that I was worth being in his arms, that he wanted to make love to Sarah and not just the latest thing that he had picked up at a party, then yes I would have been in his arms and welcomed him in me.

Instead, I was treated like shit by an arrogant bastard and I wasn't having it – not then, not now, not ever!

For all my faults, I was Sarah Bersham and I was proud of it.

So I said to Polly, "Well - we didn't hit it off. I don't think that I was his type…" and then I hesitated very slightly but had to say, "and he certainly wasn't mine."

Polly was quiet and then said, "Yes, I get it."

The conversation was only going to get worse. Polly had done her best for me and I was grateful, so I said, "I'm working from home today and I've got a killer job list. Can I phone you later?"

Like I said, Polly hadn't been given her success on a plate and she was super-tuned in to what was not being said.

"I'm off to a conference in New York tomorrow – loads of work and all that. But we'll speak when I get back.

"Love you lots."

"Love you too," I said. "Bye," and blew a kiss down the phone.

*****

The following day I went in to work and no-one noticed anything: it was cat herding as normal.

In one of the quieter moments I sent an e-mail to my boss Marcus and asked to see him.

Paige, his PA, sent back the standard response saying that he was busy/in meetings/having a pedicure/blah, blah, blah but I insisted.

Ten minutes later I got an e-mail to come up in an hour. Marcus was a floor above where I worked and I rarely saw him. It was where the people, and things, happened which kept the business running – Accounts, HR and all the serious stuff – and miles away from the manic call centres in the rest of the building.

Paige was waiting for me when I went in and as we walked the length of the floor to Marcus' office, no-one even looked up. Regardless of their age, these were grown-ups doing adult work and someone they didn't know was an irrelevance to them.

Marcus had a real office, with a proper door, a personal desk for him and a ten place meeting desk too. As I said, this was the where the adult work was done.

Paige made a superficial knock on the door and we went in. There was another woman sat against the wall behind Marcus with her iPad open and a paper note-pad on her lap too: very old school.

Marcus barely looked up from his computer screens. When he did, the look he gave me made it clear that I was nuisance and whatever I had to say needed saying quickly – and then for me to get out even faster.

This suited me just fine because I'd thought about what I was going to say a lot. I'd written my little speech about a million times in my head, beginning with a version which thanked the company for the wonderful opportunities they had given me, how grateful I was and that it would be wonderful if I could come back in a few months.

It was lies from start to finish: utter bollocks and I was finished with lying to anyone – even to me. Another version had some thanks in it and a wish that the company did well.

Then Marcus' look refined this to what I was about to say. Marcus glanced at his screen for a final time, I'm sure to check that he'd got my name right, and then spoke. "Good morning," and there was a slight pause because I don't think that his lips had ever produced the word Sarah before, "Sarah."

"This is Michelle from HR…" And he nodded to the woman sat against the wall, "and you know Paige, I'm sure."

"How can I help?" and he made a sort of grimace, like a baby with wind, which I think was to signify he was smiling – or maybe he did have wind.

I sat up straight. What had happened with Florian had really got to me and, bizarrely, had cleared away a lot of the superficiality which had been cluttering my life. I was in a mood where I wanted to tell the whole bloody world that it could fuck off and leave me alone. Just go!

Even so, my mum and dad had drummed good manners into me and they came out now.

"Marcus, I'm sorry for the drama but I have to resign – now. I've always done my best for you but I need to go soonest so I can't give you a month's notice. I'm not going anywhere else – I've just got issues that need dealing with."

I watched Michelle furiously make written notes rather than tapping away at her iPad.

"I'm sorry, but that's how it is."

Marcus said, "Well, I'm really sorry to hear that, Sarah. Is there anything we can help with?"

I'd done management training too so that was the first box ticked at the Employment Tribunal.

"Did you offer to provide support to Ms Bersham?"

"Yes we did – and here's the evidence."

Marcus grimaced again, but now with a veneer of care. I'm sure he'd been on a course teaching facial expressions.

"Is there a problem you'd like to share?"

Michelle was frantically writing all that was said between us.

No - there isn't, Marcus. No - I don't want to tell you that I've been called a frigid cow by my co-workers. Yes - I'd refused to have sex with a teenager who was leering at my wet tits. And even more no - that I'm here because some millionaire bastard tried to use me as a cheap date and… I felt the tears coming and so I sat up even straighter. I wouldn't be beaten.

"Thanks for your support Marcus, but I need a break just to get myself together.

"Everything is fine at work but I need to get my personal life sorted out."

"Okay, if that's your final decision we can only respect it."

And another big tick goes in the Employment Tribunal box.

"We've been very happy with the work your team has done so we will do the best that we can, but we're limited in how much we can do to help."

The giant marker made another tick on the check list in the sky. Marcus turned to Michelle.

"Michelle, can you tell Sarah what we can do?"

She'd been on the face mangling course too.

"Sure Marcus.

"Well, we need to be sure that there is nothing that we can do, in any way, to help you at the moment?"

"No thanks. I'm sure."

And the guillotine blade fell.

"We'll pay you for the hours you've worked, and any unused holiday entitlement will be included in your final payslip.

"Beyond that, there's no additional settlement—you forfeit notice pay by resigning without giving prior notice..."

And that was that. No box of chocolates and a cheap card signed by my team. I was out.

Marcus straightened a few papers on his desk, avoiding eye contact.

"I'll make sure HR processes your P45 promptly.

"Good luck, Sarah.

"Paige will take you down to collect your personal possessions and then you can leave as soon as you wish.

"Please don't try to log on to our network now."

He made another ghoulish fake smile and everyone stood up.

CHAPTER SEVEN

It's surprising, actually a bit frightening, to find out how much time there is in a day when you don't have to go to work, log on from home or you're not on holiday.

The first few days were okay. The outstanding holiday pay from SCC had put money into my account, but I soon found out that there are a lot of hours in the day – and every one of them is long!

I did all the little jobs around the house that I'd been putting off for ages and cleaned it like it hadn't been done for years.

I've only got a tiny garden so I did some weeding and planted two "Busy Lizzies" from the supermarket as a joke. They wouldn't have been called "Slaving Sarahs" because Sarah was getting lazier and lazier every day!

Netflix in the day was good for a week and WhatsApping people I hardly knew filled in some time but then I started to go out, just for a break from being in.

One day I drove to Mow Cop and walked up to the castle. It isn't a real castle but a summer house built a couple of hundred years ago, to look like a ruined castle and it's perched right on the edge of Mow Cop: you can see for miles.

It'd been on the news that Jodrell Bank could look back billions of years, right to the actual start of time, and I wondered if there was another Sarah out there, somewhere in the universe, feeling as empty as I did.

Then I smiled to myself at the thought. Some poor sod like me having all her dozens of boobs being messed with by a ten armed monster called Florian.

In a funny sort of way, it made me feel a lot better.

But the fact that I'd had a laugh at Alien-Sarah's problems, and that I was bored out of my mind, caused a mistake that I immediately regretted.

*****

On the way back to the car park, my phone buzzed to say that I'd got a text.

It was a long one - from my friend Marianne.

I had been close friends with Marianne at Uni and I'd kept in touch with her ever since. We'd sometimes met for meals and even occasionally had a girls' weekend away but, each year, we'd sort of drifted further apart without really knowing it.

Marianne had met an English property developer who she said owned most of the Algarve. He'd done really well after the financial crisis of 2008 and properties were on sale in Portugal for next to nothing.

He was smart, and got a Portuguese residency visa before Brexit, and so he did even better as the Brits bailed out of their villas at fire-sale prices.

They'd had a spectacular wedding in the Lake District because Marianne came from that part of the world and her Gran and Grandad didn't want to fly to Portugal. So Henry – that was her husband's name – hired the Inn on the Lake for three whole days, and she was married on the banks of Ullswater in a little white pergola.

Her dress was a brilliant white and she had a crown of little white flowers. She was just so lovely and Henry was tall, with a neat beard, and looked just like he should have done.

I was glad that I stood towards the back, where I wouldn't be noticed, in case someone thought that I was a waitress.

Like everything else, the weather was incredibly wonderful with clear blue Lake District skies which looked as if they had been scrubbed spotlessly clean, especially for the wedding.

As they walked back to the hotel, hand in hand, an RAF jet zoomed down the lake on a training flight. Henry said he had organised it just for her – which he hadn't – but everyone clapped and it was great.

*****

I wasn't jealous of Marianne but her wedding was wonderful. I still sort of dreamed about marrying a really nice man and looking lovely after a makeover and all that sort of girly stuff, instead of what that bastard Florian had tried to do.

Brandon had just moved in with me on one day and almost without me knowing - just because everyone was pairing up, so I didn't even get a registry office marriage and a meal in the pub afterwards.

After the wedding at Ullswater, Marianne and Henry had a big reception in Lagos – the Portugal Lagos, not the one in Nigeria.

I was invited but to be honest I just couldn't afford it. The hotel would have been free but I couldn't bring a £4.99 box of Quality Street to a party like that and then there were the flights and taxis and clothes I wouldn't wear again so I used work as an excuse – and this was sort of true.

After Uni, I couldn't find a permanent job so I worked at a big food bank as an unpaid volunteer. Eventually, they offered me a full time position. The pay wasn't good – it was crap actually – but I enjoyed helping people who were really struggling. I got to deal with the big supermarkets, trying to get food they were going to throw away. This was really satisfying and I was good at it.

On the back of this, I got the job as a manager at the call centre and I really had thought that I was on my way.

I had a proper partner like everyone else – Woohoo! Pin my 'Clever Girl' badge on! – and a job with prospects and I was a bit ambitious. If only I had known what a joke the whole thing was!

But now, I was sat in a great big pile of cow poo with no idea what to do next. Well, that's my excuse…

Marianne's text said that she was going to have a big party – and with Marianne I was sure that it would be big with a capital B – to celebrate her fifth wedding anniversary which had some sort symbolism and about wood, or trees or something.

With the sort of men I found, my fifth anniversary would have probably been "Bag For Life" or "Bin Recycling".

I should have said no but I was fed up and empty and so I agreed. It was no more complicated than that…

*****

I knew that I'd made a huge mistake when I saw the sign. "M56 closed for essential roadworks. Follow the diversion."

A tear came in the corner of one eye too. It wasn't the stress of having to find my way to Manchester Airport, being late and probably missing my bloody flight! No, nothing like that. When I was in the Call Centre, I spent all day every day dealing with problems. No, the tear came from not wanting to be here at all and every bloody thing going bloody wrong – again!

I hadn't wanted to get up when the alarm went off in the middle of the night and now I didn't want to be driving down the M56 at 4am.

Marianne's marriage had been perfect and now she lived in a giant villa overlooking the sea. They had a gardener and two full time staff who cleaned and even cooked. Like I said, it was perfect.

My good luck had been finding a really nice ski jacket at 70% reduction in the sale at Cheshire Oaks so at least I didn't look like a total down and out.

I just hoped that she didn't recognise the rest of my outfit, which was largely from Matalan.

I blundered my way through the zillion signs and one way roads at the airport, with the rain bouncing off the car so hard that I could hardly see.

After what seemed like hours I found the Long Stay car park.

I dragged my case out of the car and half ran down the long entry lane and out into the rain - and just stood there, desperate not to go the wrong way and be even later for my flight.

What I needed was a great big sign saying Terminal 1 This Way, with an enormous illuminated arrow - but there wasn't one. If you're stressed and late you don't need any more problems.

But there was a bloke, walking with his shoulders hunched and his head buried in his hood, towards what I thought might be the terminal.

It was getting later and later and my jeans were already soaked so I took a chance.

"Hiya. Is this the way to Terminal 1, please? They said the car park was right next to the Terminal but I can't see which way to go."

From underneath the hood a voice said, "It's sort of near the car park but not next to it. They're not going to tell you that it's a real trek before you get there – especially in this weather."

I looked up a bit through the rain, and it was stinging heavy now, and said, "Thanks. I think that I'm late already, what with this "Get there three days before your flight crap."

I looked to the right, where the traffic was coming from, and pulled my case.

Then the wheels got stuck in a massive rut so I gave the case a really hard jerk and it flew out of the hole where it was stuck and right into a giant puddle.

Oh bloody, bloody, bloody hell!

The hood said, "You okay?"

The question was asked hesitantly. This wasn't the time, or the place, to be offering unasked for assistance to a woman.

"Yes, thanks."

I thought, I'm not taking help from some stranger. I look after my own life and I can pull my own case, and get it out of a puddle without the help of some bloke with his head hidden inside a red coat.

I tried to lift the case out of the puddle with the handle but as I stood it up the wheels got stuck again.

Why now you bloody wheels? Why can't you just do your job and go round and round?

I hate airports and the rain and the dark - and every bloody thing else!

The bloke was still there. He said, "Here let me give you a hand – if that's okay…"

He wiggled the wheels of the case out of the pothole, they came free and he handed the case back to me.

Now what to do? He'd not only helped but I'd let him help.

What was he going to think of me?

I had an idea. It wasn't one of my best ever ones but it was dark and I was soaked, so I pretended that he hadn't really helped and turned it all into a joke.

"Thanks. A real knight in wet red armour. Where's your horse?"

He just smiled. I could see that the joke, crap though it was, had avoided what he really dreaded – him coming across as pushy and taking advantage, whatever advantage is, of woman at five o'clock in the morning, in the pitch black and pouring rain.

Christ! That was only one step away from a sexual assault.

He played the joke hard so that I knew that all he wanted to do was get the suitcase wheels out of the pothole and on to the less flooded pavement.

"It's a good job that the hole wasn't any deeper. You would have had to go swimming to find it."

"I'm going to Terminal 1 - it's along here."

"Thanks. You should get a job as a tour guide," and immediately regretted it.

It sounded such a real smarty-pants' comment so I smiled a little bit and hoped that he saw it from inside his hood.

*****

We carried on walking in silence, our heads down against the driving rain.

I wanted to say something because he'd been kind – actually kind twice.

First, he had given me directions and then he'd saved my case but there was nothing that I could say which wasn't smart-arsey again or, worse still, too friendly to some strange bloke who was on the way to meet his girlfriend - or wife or boyfriend or on the run from the police for not paying parking fines or who was looking for women who were lost at Manchester Airport at five o'clock in the morning.

Inside my hood, I giggled at that last idea. There had to be a lot better places to go for a molest than the cold and sloshing rain of Manchester Airport.

My ski jacket was good, and covered a bit of my bum, but my legs were soaked and cold by the time we reached the terminal. That's my excuse for almost stepping out into the road, right in front of a taxi.

He sorted of shouted quietly, can you both shout and be loud at the same time?

"Whoaa! Steady. That taxi driver'll charge you if dent the front of his car."

I looked up and said, "Thanks. That's all I need."

It was enough to say but for half a second, no - probably less than that, I had the thought that someone had looked out for me.

I'd come through a lot and I was still here. I didn't need anyone to do anything for me, not ever, but just for that flash someone had taken care – for me, and for nothing, just because they wanted to.

It was weird.

We crossed the road and went into the terminal building. He was still standing near me, not near me like near, but a bit near, when I asked one of the security guards if they knew where the check-in for Faro was.

He'd taken his hood down by this time and I saw that he had thick, curly brown hair and what I call smiling eyes. He smiled at me – and I wished that he hadn't, because I didn't want to get in a conversation with him. But he did have a lovely smile.

The guard said, "Next floor love. Up the escalator and keep on going and you'll see TAP right at the end.

Now I had my handbag and my big suitcase - the one which had tried to drown itself ten minutes before – and was trying to squeeze through a gap on the escalator when I knew that I should have gone in the lift. And he just stood there patiently waiting. Well, probably patiently.

I didn't even want the bloody suitcase but I couldn't spend five days with the wife of a zillionaire and wear the same top and jeans all the time, so almost every bit of decent clothing I owned was in the wet plastic case.

I backed up - and the suitcase ran right over his foot. Bloody hell! I just couldn't imagine what was going to go wrong next. This was such a rotten trip.

"Oh. I'm sorry. Have I run over your foot? It's this case. It's a big lump and the wheels aren't very good.

"But you already know that…

"I should have been sensible and used the lift."

He smiled again. "That's no worry. These escalators are always a nuisance.

"Do you want a hand?"

He stood well back so that he wasn't crowding me.

I said, "Thanks that'd be great. You've got to be so careful now what with the weight and size and everything.

"I had to measure it really carefully because you're only allowed so much and I didn't want charging extra if it was too big or heavy."

The ideas wouldn't come out of my mouth in an orderly way and tripped over themselves like some infant demanding a toy, but not knowing the right words to ask for it.

"It was the same with my handbag."

I weakly waved my big Scotch Plaid, Barbour handbag – Cheshire Oaks' sale again – to prove the truth of what I was saying, as if he needed or wanted any further evidence from a woman he had only just met and who couldn't stop talking.

"The bag is going with me in the cabin and you know how strict they can be over these."

My voice tailed off…

"When I went to Spain my handbag wouldn't quite go through the measuring thing so I had to take my purse and hair brush out and put them in my fleece pockets and the girl still looked at me as if I was a drugs' dealer."

Then I wished that I had shut up instead of going on but he was still smiling so he probably wasn't going to text security and get me chucked out of the airport.

"BBC North-West Tonight reports that a 34 year old woman was arrested at Manchester Airport for boring the pants off a bloke."

But he didn't seem as if he was going to report me.

Instead, he smiled again and said: "I know what you mean. I push the stuff around in my back pack, if they check, to get it flat but you do have to be so careful.

"Where you going today?

"Whoops! Watch out for that escalator step sticking…"

Was it any of his business whether I crashed in a big heap at the end of the escalator - or should he have just kept his nose out?

That's what should have been in my mind – but it wasn't.

Instead, the same terrible thought hit me again – and I do mean hit – just as it did when I nearly walked into the taxi: somebody cared.

I couldn't say just nothing so I thought that I'd go for a few plastic words which would fill the gap like the packing on a parcel – just something to fill the space and stop the embarrassment from rattling about too much.

"I'm going to Faro. It's my friend from Uni. She's having a big party to celebrate five years of being married. I don't really want to go because I can't afford it, but she's been asking me to see her villa in Portugal for ages now so I can't escape."

That was too much to say to someone I didn't even know but the words somehow had left my mouth before I could stop them.

The big hood-man smiled again. He never stopped. "I'm going to give my mate a hand. I don't want to go either. He works with tourist charter boats and they're taking them all out of the water for the winter.

"He knows that I've just been made redundant, and he's done me loads of favours, so I couldn't really say no."

Now he'd told me a lot more than he should have: that meant we were equal, and I felt better.

We were stood next to each other in the queue, shuffling forward together, I mean as if we were together, and all the time he was smiling.

He never stopped smiling so, because I couldn't help it, I smiled too but I didn't want to because I didn't know him.

When we reached the desk he stood back so that I could go first.

"Can I see your ticket, please?

"Thanks."

The agent goes through all the standard checking and re-checking and even more checks.

"Passport."

He doesn't even make eye contact. He's more interested in the girl who has just walked behind him. He sort of half holds out his hand without looking at me.

The bloke who I'd found, or maybe who'd found me, was now standing quite close so I slid my passport across the check-out desk, almost face down like a card player.

"My" bloke seemed very pleasant but I didn't want him to see my name or anything in case there was a weirdy hiding inside his big jacket.

"Hold luggage?"

"Yes."

The case wasn't heavy so I got it on the scales without any trouble.

"My" bloke just looked on.

The other bloke, the one at the desk, was far more interested in the girl who had walked back past the other way. She smiles at him – and not just a matey smile either. No wonder he couldn't keep his mind on checking in passengers.

He scribbled something down, printed a label, threaded it round my suitcase handle and the conveyor belt gave a bit of a rumble and a burp – it must have had a Vindaloo for its tea last night – and my bag disappeared.

At last the check-in bloke looks up and actually makes eye contact. He slides my boarding pass across the desk and says, "Okay, you can go straight to security.

"Have a good trip…"

But his interest had disappeared again because the see-you-later-for-a-drink girl was back for another walk by visit.

He turned to… I don't know who, so I continued to think of him as "My bloke" not because he is my bloke any more than a bag of crisps becomes your crisps if you find them on the pavement. They're just crisps that you have come across.

"You going to Faro too, Sir?"

"Yes."

"Carry on?"
"Yes. No big stuff today."
"That way then."

*****

I could have just walked off the moment that my bag was checked in but he smiled at me again and we were both going to Faro and he'd helped me and so I hesitated and that's how I found myself walking not alongside him, not with him or anything, but sort of near him – but not near if you know what I mean.

His rucksack was faded and well-worn so it had obviously been to a lot of places. He carried it easily just with one strap over his shoulder.

I know that this sounds really strange but he looked comfortable with the big bag and the bag looked as if it was happy to be with him. They both looked as if they were telling the truth about each other.

It was quite a long walk from check-in to security and we didn't speak. In the end, I was getting embarrassed so I said, "I always hate security in case the alarm thing goes off.

"I'm not wearing any jewellery so I don't get buzzed but I know I'm going to have to take my shoes off because they've got a little metal buckle."

He stopped so I did too. Then he had a proper look at my shoes.
"They're nice."

And I thought that he actually did like them.
"Thanks. They're really comfortable for walking around and I can slip them off on the plane really easily."

We carried on walking together, and not together, to present our boarding passes at the automated check-in machine.
"You first."

I was admitted without any issues but he struggled.

"Oh, the thing won't work. I can never get the self-checkout to work at supermarkets either."

I said, "You have to put your boarding pass exactly flat and then it'll work." I felt a tiny bit pleased that I could do something to help him.

"Thanks. My mum says that I could do with a full-time carer."

*****

The barriers opened and we went through and joined the end of the long queue for security. It was a really strange experience and I wasn't handling it well, being with him but not being with him even a little bit. No, not even one tiny bit!

It was as if I knew the bloke but didn't know him at all. I mean, he'd rescued my suitcase from that huge puddle and walked me to the Terminal but he didn't really walk me there, like walking me back to my car after a date, he just walked with me.

Then he did get my bag onto the escalator but that's what anyone would do for someone who was struggling, except that I wasn't struggling – or maybe I was because I'd just run over his foot.

And I'd told him about going to Faro and he'd told me about going to work on a boat.

So, we'd both given bits of information but nothing really. I'd not even asked his name and he hadn't asked mine so there was still a nice, big, high wall between us.

He turned to me and smiled – all the time a gentle, reassuring, happy smile as he took off his coat and put it into the big grey tray.

"I feel as if I'm getting undressed now.

"Watch, belt, phone."

I saw his flat belly and for less than half a second, no - less than that, had the terrible thought that seeing him undressed might not be a such a bad experience.

Then I squashed the idea flat and forever.

I said, "I hope that I don't get bleeped."

I didn't add that I had made sure that I wasn't wearing an under wired bra which normally sets off the alarm.

I'd have died a death if the security lady had waved her wand round and round my boobs while my bloke looked at me.

No, no, no. Not my bloke at all. While some bloke I didn't know, and would never know, looked at me with my hands held high whilst my boobs were tested for explosives.

Our boxes popped out of the scanner next to each other. Mine with my wet coat and big Barbour handbag in it and his following, piled high with his rucksack which someone had squashed flat.

He scooped up my tray and put it in the area away from the conveyor belt, just as you would for a friend.

It was one of those 50/50 situations that are always coming up. Was he a pushy, cheeky sod for touching my tray when he didn't know me or was it just good manners, like people used to have for each other?

He took his big rucksack out of his tray effortlessly and then turned to smile at me again.

Why me? Look bloke, can't you just bugger off now and leave me alone to think how I am going to make my money last for five days?

But he did smile – and then things got much, much worse.

"We've been really quick through security so do you fancy a coffee before we go to the gate for our flight?"

The offer of coffee was bad enough but then he'd said that WE, yes WE, were going to go the gate for OUR flight.

There were loads of ways out of this and I could have taken any of them.

I had to text my brother and check if my mum was okay – a good one, even if I didn't actually have a brother.

Then I had to check my e-mails – which was sort of true.

Or even the final solution. I needed the loo – and might be some time. No man ever presses you about the time you need on the toilet.

But he smiled and so I said the worst possible thing. "Thanks. That'll be lovely."

And then we walked together into the lounge.

Was this is a bad as things could get? No, there was much worse to come. I liked walking with him.

He'd been kind and not pushy, and there was always his smile.

There were loads of places selling coffee and I didn't know what to do – whether to let him choose or make a suggestion.

I was also getting worried about him only drinking de-caffeinated, vegan, spring water coffee so my mind flicked to the off switch and how I could escape.

But all that he said was, "There's a Starbucks. You can't go wrong with them."

And he didn't ask my opinion but we walked together, but not together, just as we'd been doing all the way from the Long Stay Car Park.

He found an empty table on the outside of the café and said, "This okay?"

I mumbled something and sort of smiled.

"What'd you like?"

"Oh no, I'll get them. I mean you've done enough already rescuing my case from that lake and…"

My voice trailed off remembering how much he had really done for me.

He said. "Tell you what. You can buy the second cup."

And he smiled a really deep, friendly, trustworthy smile.

"How about that?

"What would you like?"

I said, "A skinny latte, please."

"I'm having a flapjack. I always have a decent breakfast and I'm starving now.

"So, what'd you like?"

I smiled as well. It was difficult not to. "I'll have a chocolate muffin, if they've got any. I should be dieting but today's the wrong day!"

If I'd still been on the little black dress diet and I would have said no – but I wasn't. That was in the past and now I was in faded jeans and baggy top mode.

He got up and went to order – for us both.

*****

Even now, it's difficult to describe how I felt because it wasn't one of those giant emotional moments like when I'd chucked Brandon out of my house – and I really do mean that I chucked him out, because he'd ended up in a big heap in Mrs Tunstall's garden.

It wasn't as if I'd had never had a boyfriend either. I'd even lived with one for a bit in my second year at Uni. That was Dave, who played badminton for his County and was very sporty.

Michel, the chef who worked in the Black Greyhound pub, was good fun too but worked crazy hours so we never got to know each other properly.

Then there was the slog, and it really did feel like hard work, of "More Than Friends" and picking up the broken pieces of men who'd already had a life and were now looking to re-build after the earthquake which had destroyed it – and there were a lot of them!

Of course, there were plenty of blokes out there who were cheap versions of Florian and I wasn't having this either. I wanted someone to want to be with me for more than just seeing me in bed.

What was missing, even if they ticked every box, was that I never felt that I could be really me with them, that I could just be myself – whatever that was. Somehow, there was always that little empty space that needed filling.

Now, my bloke had gone to get us coffee and I actually wanted him to come back and sit with me. Not for anything, but just to be with me because I liked him.

This was mad – absolutely bonkers. I didn't even know his name and he could have a wife and three kids or be a drugs dealer or some bloke just on the look-out for what all blokes want.

But my bloke hadn't been wearing a wedding band, or even any sign of where a wedding band used to be. Believe me, by the time you get to 34 you get really good, and very fast, at spotting this.

He also seemed too honest to be two timing, or three timing, anyone and even if he was married or had a partner or whatever, what was wrong with having a coffee with someone he'd met in a security queue?

So I got my phone out and sent a text to my mum to say that I'd arrived in plenty of time and that everything had been great and now I was having a coffee – with a bloke whose name I didn't know just because he'd been kind to me.

Except that I didn't say that - but stopped when I got to the "having a coffee…" bit.

Then I looked at the weather for Lagos and it was great – sunny and 24. A bit of sun on my arms and legs would be incredible and pay me back for the expense of the trip.

My bloke came back with a tray. On it were two coffees, my muffin, his flap jack and two napkins. He took my coffee and the muffin from the tray first put them on my side of the table.

Then we looked at each other for what seemed like ages.

He raised his cup and said, "Cheers" then he smiled and took a long drink.

"Look, because we seem to be spending a lot of time together," and he laughed out loud "do you think we ought to know who we're talking to?

"I'm Adam…" and he sort of held his hand out towards me and smiled.

I took it but felt like a real girlie. I normally have a firm handshake but the one I gave was all soggy.

"Pleased to meet you. I'm Sarah."

He took another drink and I could almost see the gears whirring away in his mind working out what to say next because it was his turn in this conversation tennis match.

"Well, like I said before I'm going to help my mate who works for a yacht charter company in Lagos. Normally, I mend trucks but the firm I was working for is getting everything done in Poland now and so they don't need British technicians, and they don't want a British garage either.

"I got a pay-off but this can soon go - so I only needed a bit of persuading to go and help with the boats and get a few quid and free meals.

"What about you?"

So I told him all about Marianne, and the jet flying down the lake when she had got married and how the M56 was closed and I had to drive half way round England to get to Manchester Airport.

It all came tumbling out but I didn't feel awkward or anything because Adam – now I knew his name this felt so much better – joined in and sounded interested and best of all, added bits of things to my stories so it felt like a conversation between two friends.

Then I offered to get us both a second cup of coffee. I could see him from the counter while I was waiting and I was pleased to be going back to him.

Wow! That was properly odd.

*****

We sat sipping our coffee and, I have to be honest, just enjoying being with each other. I had a little silent giggle at how he tried to creep up on the subject of whether I was in a relationship and catch it by surprise so that it didn't know it was being hunted.

Of course, it did know – and I did too.

So when he said did I have anyone I could have taken with me to Lagos I said no, I didn't and although I had lots of friends (which was a bit of fib) there was no-one special, like that sort of special.

Then the ball came over my side of the net but I was a bit more direct and asked him was there anyone waiting for him in Lagos in a bikini, like all sailors have.

He laughed and said that the deck crew got all the girls in bikinis but the engineers were always too grubby to attract the ladies.

Eventually, he looked at his watch – yes, he did have a watch, one of those divers' things with a blue ring round the outside – and said: "We'd better be making a move because they board early these days.

We'd better be making a move? What we? He was nice and friendly but my next five days were going to be as full as his.

Then some Superhero God decided to have a laugh.

He looked at his ticket and said, "What seat are you in?"

I got my ticket out and said, "I am sitting in 8A. It's near the front so I can get off pretty quick when we land."

He looked at his ticket and said, "I've got 8B.

"That's really is freaky. We're sat next to each other."

And then he really grinned, "And you're not allowed to change seats unless you feel threatened.

"Do you feel threatened sitting next to me?"

This was getting really, properly soppy. That's my excuse for what I said next.

"No, I don't feel threatened. I'd really like to sit next to you."

*****

I suppose that this would be a better story if we walked hand in hand and talked about really important things like whether the war in Ukraine would spread, or global warming or something like that.

But we didn't. Adam asked if I wanted anything from the shops, without actually saying scent or soap, and I said that I couldn't afford anything from shops which sold Chanel, Gucci and Armani.

When we came to the wine and whisky it was me who asked him what he wanted but he said there was so much booze left on boats by clients that he could be an alcoholic in a week and in any case, he wasn't fussed over drink one way or the other.

When we got to the sweets section, I said: "I really fancy some chocolate for on the plane.

"What do you like?"

I was buying chocolate for us, not for me, and that was really weird again.

Adam said he liked fruit and nut which was a relief because I did too. I bought a packet of little bars of chocolate so we could have our own — sort of sharing in matey sort of way but not proper, "Let me break a piece of my choccy off for you."

Afterwards we walked on and I found the gate on the display board where we were supposed to be. I pointed it out to Adam. He didn't say anything, nothing at all. He just followed me as I set off.

I keep saying that things were getting worse every second — and they were.

Adam stopped outside one of the toilets and said: "I'm going to go now because the plane we're flying on is only small.

"The last time that I flew with TAP Airlines they only had one toilet for passengers in the cheap seats. By the time we got Faro I was bursting so I'm going to get a visit in now."

Now to the worst of the worst.

Everywhere was packed with people and there were no seats anywhere so I said, "I'll wait here for you."

I then I realised the giant thing I'd just said. I had offered to sit with my bum against a row of seats waiting for a man whose name I didn't even know an hour before.

I'd dug a monster hole and couldn't climb out so the mad part of my brain said: "If you want, I'll mind your bag."

Not that he couldn't use the toilet with his rucksack on his back, it was just that I wanted to do something for him – something to show that I wanted to be more than a girl who couldn't stop talking and whose case he had rescued.

There were no right words but I hoped that he could see what I was offering.

He said thanks and put the bag down on the floor, touching my left foot, and then he went into the toilets and I watched him go, as if we had been married ten years.

When he came out he said, "That's better. Maybe I'll get to Faro without a visit..." and smiled that lovely smile.

"It's three hours and with only one toilet for all the discount passengers I'd have been in a right state after two cups of coffee."

And he paused and didn't pick up his bag. It was like being on the far side of a bridge and you can see that someone is waving to you and their mouth is moving, but you can't hear what they are saying.

But I did know what this man was saying to me, outside the toilets on the way to Gate 72 at Manchester International Airport.

He was saying, "Look if you've got any common sense you'll go now while you can otherwise you're going to have a problem.

"And I've thought about this and I'm trying to be kind, like I was before, but I can't just come out and mention toilets."

He said all this in the few seconds of silence as he looked at me.

The right thing to do would have been to ignore the cheeky sod. How long I could go without a pee was nothing to do with him and he should mind his own business. But no matter how hard I tried, we seemed to keep banging into each other and, every time, we got a tiny bit closer and stayed together longer.

So I went and he didn't stare at me or anything but just got his phone out straightaway. As I turned right into the ladies, I risked a quick look back and there he was, with a few other blokes waiting for their wives or girlfriends, looking at his phone and not even texting. My God. It was if we were a couple.

There wasn't a queue but I took my time in the cubicle because I needed to clear my head.

Then I stood washing my hands, over and over. There was a tall girl, with big earrings, stood next to me and I saw her having a quick look at me soaping my hands again and then spending ages rinsing them. I bet she thought I'd got some mad OCD where I had to get my hands spotlessly clean.

I didn't care and just carried on washing while I thought. I was stuck with Adam for the next three hours but that wasn't much of a problem. When we got on the plane, I'd just text a load of people and then read some stuff on my phone.

We'd have to say a few words to each other but he'd soon get the idea and leave me alone. Then we'd be in Faro, I'd never see him again and that would be that.

Then I thought of how kind he'd been and how we'd talked like friends who really knew each other when we were having coffee.

Then there was his smile and how he couldn't get his boarding pass to work and I'd showed him how, and when he'd looked at my shoes and said that he liked them, and the way he looked at me without anything being hidden.

I tried not to, but I wanted to go out of the toilets and find him still there waiting for me with a smile.

I rubbed my hands round and round under the drier and felt funny things inside because I did want Adam not to have cleared off and have left me - but to be there.

And he was.

He smiled and didn't say anything about how long I'd been so I made things easier for us by saying, "Sorry I've been so long. The queue in the ladies was enormous…"

He didn't make any smart-arse comment but just smiled and

heaved his bag on to his shoulders and then said, "We'd better get a move on because they board early."

*****

So we set off through the crowds and this time we were together, and I wanted Adam to be with me as much as I wanted to be with him.

At this point in the story, he should have taken my hand and said how wonderful I looked – which would have been stretching the truth a lot – and how glad he was that he'd nearly walked into me on the pavement by the long term car park and wasn't fate, or whatever you wanted to call it, wonderful?

Except that it wasn't like this – not even a little bit.

In fact, we didn't even speak a word all the way to the gate and then the first thing that he said was, "This is packed. Let's get a seat in the next bay. We'll still be able to hear them calling our flight."

And that's what we did. He was squashed up against the wall, with his rucksack between his legs and mine, and I was trying to avoid getting crushed by a giant bloke who was going to ruin someone's flight when he sat next to them on the plane.

Then he got out his phone and looked at something so I took my phone out of my bag and started to read a recipe for spicy chicken, because I like cooking.

This lasted for about a minute and then he put his phone back in his pocket and looked at me. If what he said next was supposed to be a chat up line, he'd have been better watching more dating shows.

"Hiya. I'm Adam. Do you come here often?"

And he smiled.

The strange thing was that I knew what I wanted to say next – I was more certain than anything I'd ever said to a man before – ever, since I first realised what blokes were.

"No, I don't often come to Manchester Airport often – only when I'm going to sit next to someone really nice."

There. I'd done it. No way out and no defence if he decided that he'd had enough of girls who couldn't stop talking and were too thick to find their own way to a terminal.

What happened next would be up to him.

But he smiled and said, "I'm glad."

*****

Okay back to the romance story - which isn't either a real story, or a real romance.

By the time you actually go on a date you know, or you think that you know, a bit - or even a lot - about the bloke you're meeting.

If you're like me, you've checked that the picture he sent to you is actually him and that he really does live in Macclesfield and not in some warehouse in Russia sending out scam messages.

You've looked at his texts and mails to see if he can spell, and if he cares enough to be bothered about putting capital letters at the start of sentences – even if he doesn't know exactly what a sentence is.

I know that's the comment of a real language snob, with a 2:1 in English Lit, but it does mean a lot to me. I mean, I want to be able to talk to my date not be watching everything I say in case the words I use are too hard for him.

Then I would have found out if he only ate free range Himalayan ants, ethically cooked in virgin llama milk or whatever. I mean, everyone needs passions but I can't be done with blokes, or women, who go around shouting about them.

I would have also found out if he was a gym fanatic or ran 10 miles a day because this wasn't my thing.

Now I'm going to sound really defensive. I've nothing against girls who can go jogging without a bra but it's not for me – not at my size!

Then I'd have noticed if he cared about himself – not all designer clothes and a shirt open to show off his abs but enough to prove that he thought it was worth sending a decent picture of himself.

Really, I always looked for a bloke who felt that at least I was worth making a bit of effort for – even if nothing happened. That's how smooth talking Brandon conned his way into my life!

By the time you get to my age, you expect all men to have had a lot of relationships but I needed honesty – not one night stands because he knew that he was going to get married next month – and I've met that sort!

Of course, with Adam everything was different.

I knew nothing about him at all except that, for sure, he was kind and smiled a lot. He'd done nice things for me too many times in the last three hours for it all to be an act so I wanted...

Well, what did I want - except to talk to him just because he seemed like a really nice person?

We were getting a lot closer together, not that we fancied each other but because the huge bloke next to me seemed to be spreading himself out more and more!

I wriggled closer to Adam and he smiled. I knew what to start with: football. All blokes have a team.

"What team do you support?"

His reply was a bit odd. "Man U, I suppose." But he didn't sound very convinced.

"Who do you support?"

This was going wrong! I hardly knew any football teams but I'd seen Liverpool on the news the day before, with Arnie Slot or Bertie Blot or someone jumping up and down after the match because they'd beaten someone.

And that was about the end of my football knowledge.

So I said, "Liverpool" - but couldn't stop a giggle coming.

Adam said, "You don't really support Liverpool, do you?"

I shook my head.

"That's a relief. I hate football. I only said I supported Man U because everyone has to have a team – it's the law.

"I just can't understand what people see in football and I can't get my head around paying someone £10,000 a day to kick a football.

"I don't get it."

It was lovely that he was so relaxed and that we'd both had a laugh at us trying to do the right thing.

"Do you like any sport?"

"Yes, I love bike racing – motorbikes I mean not blokes in Lycra pedalling their bits off.

"I like the engineering as much as the racing.

"The racing is fantastic too with every lap a battle.

"It's a great show, even if you don't know anything about bikes."

There was no way back. "It sounds great but I've never had anyone to go with."

There was roaring in my ears. Honestly, the noise was like the worst storm wind you can imagine.

Look Adam, just ask me for my bloody phone number and say we can go together. Please ask me for my number – please.

But he didn't.

Except for being jammed in by the enormous bloke I'd have got up and stood by the gate because I didn't want to say another word to Adam – if his name really was Adam.

I had nothing to say so didn't say anything. I'd given him the opportunity and he'd told me to get stuffed so that was that. It was typical bloke behaviour – me, me, me, me, me.

What you want doesn't matter because there's always me.

*****

Adam stood up and looked to where the planes were parked. He pointed to one smaller than all the rest and said, "That's the Embraer jet we're flying on. It's made in Brazil."

I just don't know how he had the bare faced cheek to talk to me when I'd just all but asked him for a date, even with bloody motorbikes, and he'd ignored me.

I wished that I'd never agreed to see Marianne. Nothing had gone right and the whole trip had been a disaster right from when I'd picked up my toothbrush this morning and its battery had been flat and I'd had to have grungy teeth.

Now I wasn't upset – I was furious and, when he turned to look at me again, I could have punched him right in his fat face – except that it wasn't that fat and he really did look embarrassed.

I just turned away and he gently touched my arm. I snatched it away and now he really was asking for a smack.

"Sarah…" and there was a pause, "Sarah, just then, I didn't know what to say, you know, when you said that you'd like to see the bike racing but didn't have anyone to go with." His voice trailed off.

Even in wall of noise from the hundreds of chattering passenger and shrieking kids the silence was deafening.

"I mean, we've only just met and I didn't want you to think that I was coming on hard or stalking you or anything."

There was another immense silent space.

"Look, if I give you my number and after, when you have had a think, I mean after Marianne and this weekend, well after if you want to text me or ring or anything then perhaps we can meet up for a coffee or something?

"I'd really like that."

It was like when I was in Sixth Form and we went to the baths after school and there were some lads from another school there. I really fancied one and so I started showing off, like you do when you're sixteen, and I sort of half dived and half fell into the deep end and all the water went up my nose.

When I came up, I was spluttering and coughing everywhere and him and his mates were laughing at me.

Now, I had my head full of water again and I was choking just like at the baths and I really didn't want Adam to laugh at me, either to my face or inside where I couldn't see.

But what was really odd is that I knew that I didn't have a choice. "Thanks."

He spoke his number out loud to me, nice and slowly so that there were no mistakes and I put it into my phone.

"Would you like mine?

He just smiled that lovely smile and said, "I'll put it under Sarah Suitcase so that I'll know where it is straightaway."

When he said that, the same fear gripped me again. "Why, do you know so many Sarahs that you'd get me mixed up with someone else?"

Can someone look at you quietly? I think that they can. He didn't touch me or anything but just said, "Come on, there's a bit of space in the corridor – if you don't mind standing."

We shuffled through the packed people and found a gap behind the coffee machine, next to the window. It was a squash but there was only room for two of us so we had a bit of privacy.

"I don't know a lot of Sarahs. I don't know any except you.

"So let's get it over with.

"I'm not married and I don't have a live in girlfriend and a load of kids. I don't have any girlfriend at all.

"I did live with a girl but she was never at home and I was never at home, so we both thought, 'Why are we bothering?'

"And we didn't know.

"I came home from work one day and there was a two line note saying that she was staying with her mate and not to contact her and that was that.

"So it's just me and the goldfish – and my mum sees more of him than I do."

And this time his smile dripped sadness.

"Okay, what about you?"

He was a bit taller than me but I needed to look him the eyes so I stood up as straight as I could.

"Well, I was living with a bloke and he was in my house.

"*My* house and I'd worked hard to get a deposit for it.

"He was a teacher - he taught history in a High School. Anyway, it was going to be the big thing and he seemed really nice.

"Then I started noticing a bit of money missing from my purse – not a lot, just a bit every now and then and I thought it must be me forgetting what was there.

"I don't carry much cash but I remember that day I'd put a brand new £10 note and a £20, in, straight from the cash machine. I remember thinking how absolutely flat and perfect the £10 note was because it had never been used.

"I was making our tea and the kitchen door was open a bit but I was looking in the little cupboard behind it.

"I could see through the gap between the door and the wall, and I saw him look in the kitchen and then go in my handbag. My purse was on the top and he took the £10 note out and put my purse back, really quick.

"The thieving bastard. He was taking *my* money, in *my* bloody house – and while I cooked tea!

"I was absolutely furious and I really think I would have done something mad if I'd had my big rolling pin or scissors or something, but all that I had was a tea towel."

And I laughed.

Adam did too, which made me feel better.

"So I whacked him really hard on his ear with my fist and then I kicked him! I wished that I'd been wearing my walking boots instead of Crocs.

"And he was whinging and whining saying that he was only going to borrow the money but I'd seen that crafty look when he was checking to see if I was in the kitchen.

"He was stealing my money.

"So I opened the door and started screaming at him and battering him with my fists and he sort of fell out and into Mrs Tunstall's garden.

"I've only got a tiny little front garden and there he was blubbering like a baby and saying it was all a mistake. He was still there when I chucked his stuff at him and told him to clear off forever."

Just remembering what had happened got me out of breath and so there was a bit of break before I said, "And I've not got a boyfriend now, or a girlfriend, and there are no kids either and I don't know anyone else called Adam but I could put you into my phone as Adam Case if you don't want me to know your second name either."

He laughed a big, happy laugh and said, "Well, that's a real warning for me. I'd better watch what I say or I'll get a punch in the mouth."

I wanted to say something really nice, or funny, but it's hard to think of something that's clever but not smarty-pants when you're in a spin - so in the end I said nothing.

So there we were, squashed up right against the window and we started to talk about everything and nothing.

For a laugh at Uni, I'd been on a speed dating night – funnily enough with Marianne – and it was nothing like this.

For a start, most of the time we weren't looking at each other because there wasn't the room.

Then there were the pauses because neither of us was sure what to say, and I was getting the feeling that Adam wanted things to go right too - and didn't have any better of idea how to make this happen than me – and I didn't have a clue.

So, neither of us was in a relationship and I believed Adam. He seemed a real sort of what-you-see-is-what-you-get sort of guy.

When I was a little girl, one of my very favourite things in the world was sitting colouring in pictures with my Nanna. She had this book full of pictures of fairies and dragons and all sort of other magic stuff, and we'd spend hours choosing just the right colour for each little space.

It was just like this now. With speed dating you just get a tin of paint and a big brush and slosh it down as quickly as possible.

But now, I was colouring in all the little spaces, like I had done with my Nanna, taking great care only to do just that little shape and with exactly the right colour.

Yes, I liked walks. I liked walking along the beach at Prestatyn but I hadn't been for ages because, you know, going for a walk on your own was a bit weird.

No, I didn't like Love Island.

Even if I had the figure for it, I wouldn't have sat in almost a non-bikini so that ten zillion viewers could look at my boobs and my bum.

I didn't fancy blokes who had to spend ten hours a day in the gym to get bodies like they did either.

"Well that's a relief because I've better things to do than heaving lumps of iron around!"

Well he never actually said exactly that, but I could tell that he had no interest in gyms – and that was a relief.

He got his exercise at work, because mending trucks was quite physical, but he played badminton on a Thursday at the village hall in Willaston.

Did I know The Meadows, next to the River Dee in Chester? Well, not really because I lived near Northwich but he said that Northwich wasn't that far, was it? And they sold lovely ice-creams just by the boats and we, he really did say we, could watch the ducks and he'd bring some bread to feed them.

Now that was a proper invitation!

So it went back and to, with us both colouring in our pictures. I liked the picture I was looking at and hoped that he thought mine was okay too.

Then we heard them calling our flight.

Oh God! I was back where I'd been in Starbucks with our flight, not my flight, and there we were shuffling along together in the queue until we reached the desk. The girl looked at my passport first, then his straight afterwards, and saw that we had seats next to each other and smiled the sort of smile which we girls know exactly what it means, and said, "Enjoy your flight."

Neither of us said anything and I hoped that Adam was thinking the same things as me.

I had the window seat but I saw him sort of look towards it. This was properly scary – I mean really frightening – because we weren't growing closer together after three dates, or fifty texts but in one morning. It was like a car crash I couldn't avoid.

The worst thing of all was that I wanted to know what he wanted and...

The "and" was that I didn't know what was next because I'd never felt like this about anyone. Now I did.

I said, "Do you want the window seat?"

He said, "Are you sure? I drive a lot and I always like to look and try to see the roads that I know."

Then he laughed. "Not that I can see anything in this weather."

My jeans were still damp so I knew what he meant.

He did look out of the window but only for a bit. Then we got two new pictures out and began colouring again.

This time, the pictures were really detailed and we were colouring them in ever so carefully.

He told me that he'd been so glad that I'd shown him how to get through the security barrier and how much he hated all the taking watches and belts off crap.

Being with me, it had been the first time that he hadn't needed an extra check with the electronic wand.

And he smiled at me.

I smiled back - and then said something that I tried to pull back inside my mouth but couldn't because it had escaped before I could close the door.

"Girls have got problems too. I daren't wear an underwired bra because the arch thing would go bonkers if I did."

Bloody hell! What have I said? I wish that I could have jumped through the plane window. He knows that I wear an underwired bra - and today I'm not.

Then he had a very quick glance at my boobs and we both knew what he was thinking. He didn't stare or anything but he did look and all because of my big mouth.

He could have made all sorts of comments from something a bit smutty to outright dirty but all that he said was, "Well, as long as you're comfortable…"

And he left it at that - which was a clever thing to do as well as being kind to me. There, I've used the "k" word again.

So we carried on colouring and, as I relaxed, I got more and more tired.

*****

What happened next was properly odd – and I hope that it will explain the last part of the story.

I felt Adam very, very gently sort of touching and squeezing my arm.

He said, "Come on sleeping beauty – we're only half an hour from Faro…"

And I raised my head from his shoulder. Yes, my head from his shoulder - where it had been for God knows how long.

I'd only gone and fallen asleep on him!

Of course, with me there's always worse. Not only had my head been on his shoulder but somehow I'd wriggled round when I was asleep and my hand was sort of resting on his thigh.

He smiled at me really gently – not the big grins he'd had since the great case rescue but this time just a very soft smile. You wouldn't believe what that did to me!

Then he said, "It's been lovely having your head on my shoulder. I could feel your breath and I kept looking at you.

"I couldn't believe how lucky I was."

Then he stopped - and I waited.

"You smelt lovely too, all soft and sleepy.

"Then you wriggled round and put your hand on my leg. That was a surprise!

"This morning I didn't know you - and now, I do."

That last bit changed everything. I knew that I had fallen asleep on him but I could have got all embarrassed and stropped that my hand had ended up on his leg.

Instead it was a struggle not to cry - I was so happy.

Six hours ago I hadn't even met this bloke and now we were practically a couple.

But it did feel right. Adam was nice and if I had fallen asleep on him it was because I felt warm and safe - and it was how I had always wanted to be with a man, not watching every word I was saying and wondering if he was going to steal from me or counting the minutes until he could get my knickers off.

I felt comfortable with Adam and it was good.

The steward came round and checked that we were wearing our seat belts. Mine had sort of wriggled down between the seats and so I had to move over a bit while Adam dug it out. He didn't deliberately touch my leg or anything creepy, but I did feel his hand against my thigh. It felt completely natural, just like a couple should be - because no matter how much I tried to chase away the idea of Adam being my bloke, I wished more and more that he was.

*****

We got off the plane and walked together in silence. I had luggage to collect and he didn't so when we got to the baggage reclaim I said, "Well, see you then…

"I've got to get my case."

"No. We'll get your case together."

My case arrived in the first lot and Adam got it off the conveyor belt as if it was a toy.

We walked through the massive collection area, not speaking and with my mind going crazy wondering what was going to happen next.

The concourse was huge and there were masses of people waiting for the flights which were arriving constantly.

I said, "Just a wait a minute, please. I've got to go."

And he smiled as I almost ran to the toilets.

I was as quick as I could be but there was a queue to get in and out of the toilets and that's when it happened.

First, there was a really beautiful girl, just gorgeous, hugging Adam. Then Adam was looking towards the toilets. And last, he was pushing her away so that I wouldn't see her.

She argued for a few seconds and then went towards the shops but looking back at Adam all the time.

The next thing I remember was waking up in the medical centre with a nice Portuguese nurse holding my hand.

I'd fainted or something and I was still out when they had rescued me.

If you can imagine having all the emptiness, the sadness, the sheer waste of time just taking breaths then even that wasn't enough.

I didn't cry but just sat there like a barely living speck of dust in a giant grey cloud of nothing.

This was the end. I wanted nothing, no-one – just for it to end.

*****

Everyone was very kind and because the sadness was too much I didn't cry. I didn't have to. I just exuded so much sadness that people were kind anyway.

I said that my dad had fallen and he was very ill in hospital and might die. I got the text just as I was coming out of the toilets and this was why I had fainted.

They found a flight back to Manchester for me and in a few hours I was walking back to the Long Stay Car Park pulling my case. Just my case. No Adam, no smile – just me and my case in the rain.

I still wasn't crying but my hands were balled up in anger. Why would anyone mess with someone's emotions like he had done?

Why?

Why?

Why?

Why didn't he just ignore me?

Why did he drink coffee with me knowing that there was another woman waiting for him?

Why did he let me go to sleep on him when he was going to be in another woman's bed that night?

Just why?

CHAPTER EIGHT

Of course, the story would be better if I told you that I was a modern superwoman, shrugged him off and found another man to sleep with that night.

But I wasn't a hero. I was just me. Sad, empty beyond any words and utterly betrayed.

Why?

Why me?

What had I done in my life to deserve this? What should I tell you now to explain my sadness – my utter emptiness, my feeling of being totally alone in the world?

*****

I went home, through the road works, the rain and the traffic and just dropped my case and flopped on to the bed.

I don't know how long I lay there, honestly I don't, but when I woke up I felt like shit. I was dirty on the outside – and the inside too. I had tried so hard to be honest with Adam, and kind too, and all I got was his girlfriend or wife or mistress, or whatever she was, slobbering him with kisses the second I was gone. So I got out the gin bottle and a bag of crisps, and watched Loose Women on ITV and advice on how to get thicker lips.

Maybe Adam wouldn't have dumped me if I'd had a big injection of lip filler.

*****

It's surprising how quickly you can disappear without even trying.

I was sure that Polly blamed me for what had happened with

Florian. She'd got me a date with a handsome millionaire and all that I had to do was get into bed, fake an orgasm and live happily ever after. Except that I wouldn't have.

I changed the story with Marianne because she sort of knew my dad and I didn't want her contacting him and asking how was the stay in hospital after his fall. So I texted her and said how sorry I was that it had all gone wrong but that I needed to get back to England soonest and visit the Family Planning Clinic – and let her make what she would of that.

The truth was that I didn't care.

I didn't change my number or anything but just opted out of everything – WhatsApp groups, answering my phone and replying to texts except that to say that I'd get back to whoever, which I never did.

Very soon, I'd disappeared. I didn't want the world – and the world soon didn't want me.

*****

What didn't change were the bills.

I'd soon burnt through the money from when I walked out of the call centre and the Marianne shambles had cost me cash I didn't have.

Things really came to a head when I started paying bills with my overdraft. I can actually remember the time, the day and the place where I hit the ground – and it hurt. I woke up at 10.47 on Sunday morning with a giant hangover headache, my teeth filthy because I'd been too drunk to clean them before bed last night and smelling like chucking out time in a rough bit of Manchester.

My pyjamas hadn't been washed for a week and a rough sleeper wouldn't have looked at my bedclothes they were so bad.

There was a half empty litre bottle of gin and its best pal, the tins of tonic, on the little table next to the couch.

Like I said before, I've always been a trier and the gin bottle was the alarm call. This had to stop or I was going to be in a bigger mess than ever and in danger of losing my house because of shit blokes – and that would really have been the last straw.

This wasn't me. It wasn't. I was a bloody sight better than this. I was more angry than upset – furious with what had happened and how life had treated me – and for nothing. I wasn't going to let that bastard Florian get to me or this bloody life or my phone charger not working or anything. I'd show them!

So, I spent twenty minutes in the shower, shampooed my hair and got myself clean. Then I put my pyjamas in the washing machine along with the bed sheets.

Finally, I went to the recycling bin and dropped the gin bottle in it – and didn't even bother how much was left in it.

That was a bigger relief than I thought it would be, because it was an end to the drinking and the £20 a go attempts at forgetting how sad I was.

*****

I set the alarm for 7am and got up straight away. My head was not where it used to be but I was ready to take the first steps towards sorting my life out before I drowned in the mess. But I really did want a G&T fix. Saying you're going to give up the drink is easy – doing it is a lot harder.

First, I had to make myself presentable and then have a proper breakfast, without any gin, put on a bit of make-up, some decent clothes and find a job.

My clutch bag was at the back of the wardrobe along with the little black dress and everything else from that disastrous evening and I found the card from Mr Kumar. The phone number screamed out at me for a new start, a fresh opportunity, a car, someone who might appreciate me, who really wanted me to work for them and do well. And some decent money – and that was high on my mind.

And the Kumars were such lovely people too.

I looked at the card for a long time and then put it down.

What Florian had done had really got deep inside me. It made me question whether I was actually worth anything. So many rejections. So many failures. So many times when I really did think that things were going to be different – but then they weren't.

I just couldn't take the chance of another defeat so I put the card down and looked for an escape. Yes, an escape. No responsibility, no pressure, nobody watching me or me having to check on anyone else. Just turn up. Do what someone paid me to do, say as little as possible and go home at the end of the day.

No responsibilities. No questions asked of me – just disappear.

*****

Anyone who says that they can't get a job really doesn't want one – there are zillions out there.

I looked on Facebook pages and saw that Cheaper Than a Quid wanted staff. They always wanted staff!

I went into town and walked into their store, obviously at the unfashionable end of the high street, and asked them if they had any jobs. Gail was the manager. A big, bubbly lady in her fifties with pink hair and who obviously spent a lot of time finding people, anyone, to work for the company.

Ten minutes later, I was offered a zero hours' contract and Gail asked me when I could start.

She didn't ask me about my previous jobs, what I could do, whether I was in a relationship or anything or if I had any criminal convictions. I just had to show them a couple of utility bills to prove that I was British and entitled to work and that was that.

I came back with all the stuff they wanted and started there and then – obviously on minimum wage.

Cheaper Than a Quid was a discount version of the discount traders, and operated right at the bottom, the very bottom, of the cheap end of retailing – and I do mean at the bottom.

They made their money by selling stuff that the other discount retailers had left over – that and returns. There were odd packets of this and that, stuff in damaged boxes and things on a big shelf which had clearly been used and now had a sign, "Any Offers!"

This was not Delamere Dreams and £39 lacy bras!

But it was perfect for me.

Everyone working at "Cheaper Than a Quid" had some sort of special need. There were grannies trying to scrape a few pounds before they collected their grandchildren from school, blokes who'd got the job because their Probation Officer had done a deal with Cheaper Than a Quid Head Office and people like me - who wanted no pressure, just to get their money and go home.

There were also bonuses which Gail didn't tell me about at the start. When you got settled in, and Gail thought you could be trusted, you were allowed to see what she called, "The Skip Cupboard." This was actually a little room which had all the stuff in it that even we couldn't sell. The trust bit was that she had to be sure that you were only going to use what was in there yourself and not do something mad like try to sell it at a car boot.

There were tins of food which were so dented you were certain that they'd been dropped out of a plane, packets of pasta with the tops torn off, jeans with stains on them and once a pack of knickers which had been £5 for five until someone had whizzed two pairs and so now there were three left in a ripped packet.

They were about my size so Gail said that if I paid for something else I could have them for free. For sure, they weren't Delamere Dreams either!

So, a couple of times a week I'd take home a bag of bashed tins of tomatoes, 'Full English Breakfast in a Tin' – you wouldn't believe how awful that was – chocolate pudding and custard in another tin which looked as it had been bouncing down the M56 for a couple of miles and my favourite of all - a tea towel which said, "Today is going to be a great day" but where some poor thing in China didn't write English very well and had put "Greet" instead of "Great" day and had hyphenated "To-Day."

This just about summed up my life: wrongly spelt words and crap punctuation. It was a good dish drier though.

*****

I worked lots of overtime because the truth was that everyone else would much sooner not have been there. I didn't go out and through eating tinned food from the Skip Cupboard, and banning the gin, I soon got my overdraft under control. If you don't buy anything at all, or least anything costing much more than £1, you can really save some money.

Of course, it was too good to last. The first problem was that my diet really was unhealthy. You know that you're not supposed to eat much super-processed food? Well, I don't think that ate anything that wasn't full of E numbers and chemicals.

I even had the out of date sandwiches. White bread, 100% chemically made artificial mayo and guaranteed no natural ingredients, half a soggy bit of what was once a lettuce leaf and a tiny bit of battery chicken.

The result was that for the first time since being a teenager, I started having spots. Bloody hell. I was rotting!

Then there were the dark lines under my eyes and a skin colour which would have been great in a horror movie. I had to get a grip of this and start eating proper food again.

CHAPTER NINE

If you don't believe in fate now, I bet you will in this next part of the story – and I promise you that it's absolutely true.

Okay, so the first thing was to get some veggies and fruit bought otherwise I was going to die of super-processed fooditis.

There were regular supermarket stops for proper food on the way home but my favourite place for really nice stuff was Kintons - that mega garden centre. Gourmet food, barbecues, plants, trees and everything else you could ever want. As always, it was packed – even at six on a Saturday evening.

It's sloshing down – absolutely torrential rain and I don't have a coat with me. But it's okay. I grab a bag for life and run for the store. Buggers! I realise that I have left my handbag in the car. That's no problem because I've got my phone to pay. My handbag is out of the way, and Kintons is a posh place, so everything will be fine.

A basket of real food, and none of it out of a tin, pay at the checkout and then a pause whilst I judge the distance to my car like an Olympic sprinter waiting for the starting gun to fire.

The rain changed ever so slightly from monsoon to just torrential so away I went through the puddles to my car. I almost slid to a stop through the flood and pulled at the door handle - but nothing happened.

I tugged at it again. It can't have locked itself with the key still in my handbag – it just can't.

But it's still okay so I go round to the other side but this is locked too.

My hair is plastered all over my face and I'm raging at the car – really screaming at it and pulling the door handles as if I hated them – which I did.

I didn't even think how wet I was. There was no point. If I was only soaked to my skin, that'd be a miracle.

I raged at the bloody car again. You utter bastard car! I've always treated you properly and given you decent petrol and everything and now you've done this to me. You selfish, selfish bastard! And I actually kicked the door. A grown woman who's lost it so badly that she kicks her car door!

Then a bloke appeared from nowhere. One second he wasn't there and then he was. He was wearing a big, red jacket with a hood which covered his face. The rain was bouncing off his coat but he stood there for a moment and said, "You having a problem, love?" and he pulled the hood back a little bit.

I looked at him. "Adam!"

And he looked back at me. "Sarah!"

*****

"That girl – at Faro – the one kissing you and those hugs…

"And you sent her away so that I wouldn't see her and…"

I couldn't go on.

"My lovely Sarah. You daft thing. I could never do that to you. That was Eve – my twin sister. You know, Adam and Eve and I'm five minutes older than her.

"We're a lot more than just twins. We're best mates. We always have been. When we were little we even shared a bedroom. Eve had driven 400 miles from Gibraltar just to see me.

"Of course she was all kisses and cuddles. That's just Eve.

"And yes - I did send her out of the way, because I wanted to show her the most wonderful woman I had ever met and I wanted you to like Eve like I do.

"You know, lasers, roll of drums and the full reveal…

"Then there was a big crowd at the toilets and someone said you'd collapsed or something and they wouldn't let me be with you because I wasn't a relative and we weren't married or anything.

"And afterwards, you blocked me so I thought that I'd done something terrible and you didn't want to see me ever again.

"So I came home and every time I left the house I hoped and prayed that I'd see you again.

"And now I have."

For a moment, we just looked at each other and then went straight back in to full on hugging.

In my mind there could have been all the reasons that what Adam had said was all lies - but in my heart there wasn't: my bloke was back.

*****

Adam pushed - no that's not right, he just sort of coaxed me away from him and said, "Oh my lovely girl. I have missed you so much."

Then he looked at the car – very accusingly because he was on my side – and I told him about the warning lights and how the technician had said that the car might throw a hizzy fit and do something silly.

He was a truck mechanic and was now in full-on mechanic mode which was good but I was starting to get really cold and began shivering.

"Have you got a spare key?"

I had, but it was at home – along with my other house key too.

I told Adam and expected him to be fed up with me but all I got was another cuddle.

My wonderful man. Caring for me. Wanting to sort out my mess, for me, for nothing, just because…

Even in the driving rain I stopped myself from thinking of what the 'just because' meant.

Now he was serious.

"I don't live far from here – on the new Cable estate – so I'll take you home, dry you off and then we'll get a 24 hour locksmith to unlock your house and I'll bring you back here for your car.

"How does that sound?"

Another soppy hug was my answer.

*****

Adam didn't have a car but a big white van. He gave me an oily high vis jacket to wrap round myself and turned the heater up to full. Even then, I was shivering with the cold. Or was it just the cold?

The doubts flickered across my mind like evil Harpies, telling me Adam was lying, that the girl in the airport was really his long-time girlfriend that he was taking me back to his house for what?

Then there was Adam alongside me. Touching my thigh at every set of traffic lights; turning to smile at me; chattering about nothing and everything. My bloke from the airport. My Adam. And yes, my knight in a red jacket, riding a big white van.

He unlocked the front door and took me in to his house. Then Adam went straight into full organisational mode.

"There's the bathroom," and he pointed to the right. "It's got a really nice shower. You get warm and I'll dry your clothes on the radiator and make us a coffee."

The bathroom was bloke tidy and it was clean. This was terrible. Here I was, soaked and shivering, checking his housekeeping standards. I was actually embarrassed.

I got undressed quickly, dropped my clothes on the tiled floor and ran the shower to get it warm.

There was a knock at the door.

"Everything okay?"

I said that it was.

"Here's a couple of clean towels."

The door opened just a fraction and Adam's arm appeared holding two big towels.

I took them.

"Give me your clothes and I'll start drying them."

His arm stayed in sight.

You know one of those super-slow motion films where everything slows to almost a complete stop and the voices go all deep and blurry? Well, what happened next was worse than that - a lot worse.

I didn't answer and Adam said, "You okay?"

He even sounded a bit worried.

There was another long pause.

Then I said, "They're not all mine, honestly they're not."

Adam said, "What do you mean, not all yours? You've been out in the cold for too long."

And I could hear him laughing.

"You know, you really are bonkers. I knew that straightaway at Manchester Airport."

And he laughed again.

"Just give me your clothes, you soft thing."

So I put my Less Than a Quid work coat and my bra on his hand – and waited."

"Look, I don't want to be rude or anything, but aren't you wearing any knickers?"

But I had been. And there they were now, five for a fiver and with the one I had been given for free sat in my hand, smiling at me.

"Adam. Adam, yes of course I've been wearing knickers but they're not my knickers."

This time, he actually raised his voice.

"What do you mean, not your knickers? Has someone lent you a pair?"

So I explained and he said, "You are absolutely and totally one of a kind and that's why I love you."

Love me? He'd just pressed the nuclear button in any relationship.

He'd said that he loved me. What did that mean? What was love to him? Did he love me like I longed to be loved or was it something else? Not just sex for sure – but, maybe a weekend friend or someone to go to a motorbike race with?

Love? The word exploded in my head – with hope, with fear, with uncertainty. The ideas just whirled round and round. He did say that he loved me but he didn't even know who I was and I didn't know him either.

Can you, could you really love someone who you only know through sharing some chocolates and then falling asleep on them on a plane?

Did love at first sight ever really happen?

It was too much to hope for.

My ears screamed with the questions – and I didn't have the answers.

Please Adam, I don't want you to *promise* not to hurt me but try not to if you can.

*****

I had a long shower and even washed my hair with the shampoo which was in the bottom of the tray.

Then I dried myself off and stood in the centre of the bathroom wondering what to do next. I mean, the towels were big enough to cover me and I was sure that my clothes weren't dry yet but I couldn't go wandering round his house in towels like a girl in a romcom.

I stood at the bathroom door. "Adam. Adam! I'm out of the shower."

"That's fine. Let's get you sorted out.

"I was trying to think of what you could wear until your clothes are dry."

And the door opened just a crack again.

"Here. You can wear my swimming shorts and one of my t-shirts for a bit if you like?

"They're clean." And he was actually defensive.

So I put his shorts on and tightened the draw string so that they didn't fall down. The t-shirt was miles too big. This was great because it was so baggy that it didn't show anything.

It was very strange wearing his clothes. They didn't smell or anything – except of his soap powder – but my body was touching where his body had been – exactly where – and knowing this started to do all sorts of things to me - and without me trying.

I opened the door and Adam was there with his arms wide open.

"You look gorgeous. I like the spiky hair do. Very Goth."

He wrapped his arms right round me and held me for a long time. I felt very loved.

*****

Adam was very different from any other man I'd ever met. We had no sooner finished our latest hug, and I was beginning to think that this was all we would ever do, when he said. "You must be famished. Let me look in the freezer. I'm sure that there's a frozen pizza there."

He wasn't the only practical one in this organisation. I put my hands on my hips and faked disgust. Well, mainly I faked it.

"I'm not eating frozen pizza warmed up in a microwave!

"Haven't you got any real food?"

And I'll admit I did have a quick blush inside, thinking of how I'd been living on tins from the skip.

But this was different. I wanted to make something for Adam – for me to take things and prepare a meal.

No, that's not right – not at all. I didn't want to cook a meal for Adam and for him to say thanks, or that was nice or even you're a good cook. None of that would be right.

I wanted to make something for us. Not him. Not me. But us. The two of us because he'd used the big L word. Because Adam had told me that he loved me and now I wanted to show him that I loved him too.

There! I'd done it. I used the word which could cause so much hurt, so much disappointment because I wanted it to be true. I wanted Adam to love me – and I wanted to love Adam.

So, I opened his fridge and there were some chicken pieces already cut up. It was an expensive way of buying chicken but they were there.

I checked the sell by date. Men usually can't be trusted with sell by dates and I didn't want to kill us both with food poisoning. But somewhere in heaven an angel was on my side and they were okay.

Adam leaned over my shoulder whilst I was checking the date and said, "I was going to microwave those and have them with some rice."

I did another panto grimace. "Well, you're not now. I'm going to cook them for us."

Oh God, please don't punish me for saying that. I've said us again.

Now I was in management mode. "You said that you've got some rice? Well, weigh out 100 grams and put it in a pan and then cover it with boiling water."

He missed the significance of what I'd just said. 50 grams of rice is a good helping for one person. But I'd said 100 grams – enough for two people eating a meal together as friends do - or as a couple.

There was salt and pepper on the work surface so I salted the rice and let it bubble. Without getting all soppy, the rice reminded me of my mind with all the bits swirling round and round and not really knowing what they were doing next.

"Have you got a pan – a big frying pan?"

Adam beamed. "Like this?"

And it wasn't bad either, with a non-stick coating.

I rattled on with the list. "A wooden spoon, some tinned tomatoes and fresh ones, a chopping board, olive oil and any herbs?

"And a sharp knife?"

Adam covered his face in mock horror. "You're not going to kill me for the Faro mess?"

But I couldn't take the joke – I just couldn't so I ignored what he said and got everything ready.

"Wow! Bloody hell. You're a bit professional. Have you worked in catering?"

"No, I just like cooking - and I'm not going to let us have a frozen pizza!"

There. I'd done it again and I shouldn't have. I wasn't letting us have a frozen pizza. We, us, the two of us. A couple?

The rice was bubbling away as I stood over the cooker with Adam watching me.

There would never be a film like this on Netflix. The girl stood over the stove wearing only a baggy t-shirt and a man's trunks with a pair of his Crocs four sizes too big for her.

She is trying to concentrate on what she is doing, she really is, but he rests his hands on her shoulders and ever so gently kisses her neck and says that he loves her.

And inside that baggy t-shirt and faded swimming trunks her body loses interest in cooking anything as it trembles at his touch, his words and the thought of her feeling where he had been in the same clothes so many times.

*****

Adam had a little table in the kitchen so I told him to set it quickly if he wanted to eat. He did as he was told and put two plates out and some cutlery.

Then I said, "And have you got any white wine? I need it to finish this meal off."

"Oh yes! And now we have the winner of Master Chef in some stranger's kitchen, Sarah Bersham!" And he laughed.

And I pretended that it was funny because it would have been odd not to join in - but inside I didn't.

He had said, "Sarah Bersham."

He'd remembered my second name. After just the tiny amount of time we'd spent together he wanted to remember me.

Two hours ago I was kicking the door on my car in the pouring rain and now?

CHAPTER TEN

Adam watched me, genuinely interested in what I was doing. The little jar just said "Mixed Herbs" so I chucked these in: they'd be better than nothing.

Then I added a good slosh of the wine Adam had passed to me. It was a Chilean Chardonnay and wasn't too bad - middle of the range from a supermarket near you.

Then I had another blush inside. Oh you wine snob, Sarah Bersham. Be grateful for what you've been given – and there was a little tear deep inside me, because I was ashamed of myself.

I looked at Adam and, for a half a second, closed my eyes. "Go on. Go and sit down and wait for your tea like a good boy."

It was all so intimate, so very cozy – as if we had been together for years and years.

I drained the rice and arranged it in a circle on the plates. Then I put the chicken and tomatoes in the centre and brought them both to the little Formica table. I put his on one side and mine on the other.

Adam had put two glasses of water and two wine glasses out. All the glasses were well filled.

He held up his glass and said, "Cheers." And then there was a pause which went on for years and years and years.

"You look beautiful Sarah."

And another hesitation - which was even longer.

"I love you."

What do you say in a situation like this? Everything, every word, every gesture was going to be wrong or inadequate or hint to Adam that I didn't have the same feelings for him as he did for me so I just clinked my glass with his and said, "Enjoy".

Then I looked at my plate and began eating.

Don't judge me too harshly because that was all I could manage. And Adam did enjoy it – he really did.

He was good company too and told me some hilarious stories about being a truck mechanic. Once, he'd found a rat's nest in a truck and instead of getting all shouty and killing the creatures he'd put them at the back of a dis-used storehouse where he worked – and then checked whether they were safe the following day.

We ate slowly and shared the wine. He'd look at me, to check whether I wanted a refill, and then add a bit more and we'd chat again. It was so different from the loneliness of the gin bottle and junk food.

It was gentle, intimate and relaxed – as if I had been made to be here: and that's what my body thought too.

Then reality barged into our dinner date and I was back to being a manager.

"Adam, you can't drive me back after this much wine. If you got stopped and were over the limit it would be a disaster.

"Can you lend me the money for a taxi?"

Then I thought; how was I supposed to get in with my spare house key in the lounge cabinet and late-night locksmiths costing a fortune?

Adam must have the same thought at the same time.

"You daft thing. It would be stupid to go back home now.

"You can have my bed and I can sleep on the couch. I've got a spare toothbrush head. Your clothes will be dry in the morning – and we can have breakfast together and sort everything out then.

"That'd be much better."

And I leaned across the table and kissed him on the lips.

*****

We got up and walked hand in hand across the lounge to his bedroom. There was a single bed there with a duvet cover thrown more or less neatly across it. Everywhere there were the signs that this was a man room and that no woman and had ever been involved in it.

You can't imagine what a relief that was!

So now come the crashing waves, romantic music and the lights go dim. That's what's supposed to happen, isn't it?

Except that it didn't.

Adam kissed me again, gently and kindly. No porn kisses or groping - just very intimately, holding me close but not tight, stroking my back and my face and whispering, almost silently, how much he loved me.

I could feel him inside his jeans and so it felt very natural when he lifted up the t-shirt I was wearing and began kissing me again.

Now, I was melting – and fast too!

He tugged his belt undone and eased his jeans down and I looked at his boxer shorts which told me all that I wanted to know – and needed to know.

Then we took down the shorts I was wearing and Adam ever so gently lifted me on to his bed.

He began kissing me with care and attention and kindness – with his lips and tiny, thoughtful almost non-existent nibbles, and wonderful sips of me.

He slid out of his boxers while I looked at him and my first thought was a silent prayer that he would be gentle.

Adam spent a wonderful age kissing and caressing my tummy and touching hard against me. I floated off to somewhere else – not of this world and that's for sure – as I felt him next to me.

Then he opened my legs – always gently, always lovingly. There was nothing rushed, no urgency of just getting the act over like so many of the men I had known before.

Instead, he kissed and nibbled and sipped until I was trembling.

Then, ever so tenderly, he entered me and we made love. Yes, we made love.

How long for? I don't know. Then we came together in a climax that I thought was impossible. But it wasn't.

Afterwards, he stayed in me, kissing my neck and lips and telling me how much he loved me.

I wished that he had been there forever, and would never leave, but eventually he eased out of me.

Then he looked at me, smiled and took my left hand.

"You'd look lovely with a gold band on your finger."

I smiled too and said, "I would…"